Is the Significant Male in your life
(hereinaft
a
Take thi

1. If your SM los
   television, doe

   a. shrug his shoulders and say philosophically, "I can always get up and use the feet and hands God gave me?"

   b. start scrambling through the couch cushions, diving behind the bookcases and after missing two innings of baseball, a portion of the stock car race and the fix-it channel, all of which he had been watching simultaneously, finally contents himself with holding a calculator and watching only one channel at a time?

2. If your car breaks down, your SM will:

   a. check the tires, check the oil, check the fan belt—and when he can see nothing can be done, call roadside assistance.

   b. kick the tires, pop the hood and immediately start dismantling the engine, all the while complaining that he used to know how to fix this before they started using all of those imported computer parts.

3. If you were to ask your SM what he's thinking about, he will:

   a. give you a fond look and reply, "You, of course."

   b. blink his eyes and reply, "...say what?"

If your answers contain more than one "b" response, you've got yourself a guy!

Books by Carolyne Aarsen

Love Inspired

CAROLYNE AARSEN

and her husband, Richard, live on a small ranch in northern Alberta, where they have raised four children and numerous foster children, and are still raising cattle. Carolyne crafts her stories in her office with a large west-facing window through which she can watch the changing seasons while struggling to make her words obey.

ANY MAN OF MINE
CAROLYNE AARSEN

Steeple
Hill®

Published by Steeple Hill Books™

STEEPLE HILL BOOKS

Steeple
Hill®

ISBN-13: 978-0-373-81269-1
ISBN-10: 0-373-81269-8

ANY MAN OF MINE

Copyright © 2006 by Carolyne Aarsen

www.SteepleHill.com

Printed in U.S.A.

"...for the Lord is a God who knows,
and by him deeds are weighed."
—*1 Samuel* 2:3

I'd like to dedicate this book to all the working guys in the world: the guys who pack a lunch every day, try to get the grit out from under their nails every night and keep this world going with their ordinary work, all the while trying to figure out what a woman really wants.

Chapter One

"If I have to bounce one more quarter off of one more set of abs—" I hefted two four-liter jugs of homogenized milk onto the conveyor belt of the grocery store with a grunt "—punch one more stomach—" I followed it with two jumbo-sized boxes of breakfast cereal "—trip...over...one...more...saddle—" punctuating each word with bags of chips, peanuts and sunflower seeds "—I am going to throw an old-fashioned, fully feminine hissy fit." I glared at Tracy, who stood behind me in the line at the cash register, daring her to deny me my well-earned pique.

"Just make sure you hit high C on the scream," was all Tracy said.

As my best friend, Tracy would feign sympathy with my rants against my brothers, but I knew her heart was never fully engaged. From the first day she had come to stay overnight at the ranch and had been bombarded with my brother's spitballs as she came into the kitchen, my dad's booming voice yelling at her to come on in and join us for dinner and my mom's yelling at him to stop yelling, Tracy had fallen head over heels in love with my family.

"I still can't figure out why thirty-one-, twenty-nine- and twenty-five-year-old guys would still want to live at home," I continued, still venting. It was Tuesday morning, the second day in a week that had started badly yesterday. Today wasn't looking so good, either.

The flat tire I'd had on the way to work didn't help, nor did the fact that I'd had to change it wearing high heels and a narrow skirt on the side of a quiet gravel road.

"You still live at home and you're twenty-seven," Tracy pointed out.

"At least I, at one time, had plans to move out." I allowed a flicker of self-pity to creep into my voice.

"How is your dad?"

"The doctor said that it will be a few weeks before he's back to normal and that often people suffer deep depression after a heart attack. So I'm still hoping and praying."

Four weeks ago, my dad, Arnold Hemstead, had collapsed at the auction mart and had been rushed to the hospital. He was diagnosed with a cardiac infarction, spent ten days in the hospital and came home to three very worried sons. And me.

Neil, Chip and Jace hovered, helped and catered to my dad for thirty-six minutes, knowing that the overresponsible Danielle Hemstead—aka me—would take over, then they went back to their welding, fixing and farming.

"I caught a glimmer of my old dad the other day," I continued. "He's getting more interested in what's happening at the farm. He asked me if I was going to unload bales for Jace next week."

"Are you?"

I dismissed her comment with an exasperated eye-roll.

"Okay, I'm guessing that's no." Tracy picked up one of the magazines lined up by the counter. "Hey, here's something just for

you. Is the male in your life a man or a guy?
Take the quiz and find out."

"Guy, guy, guy and absolutely guy."

"Okay, I sense we're not done with the
sisterly pique yet." Tracy straightened the
magazine and tilted me a grin. "So, of your
dad and brothers, who rates the last outburst."

Growing up with three brothers who
reveled in their "guyness" gave me lots of
ranting fodder, but Tracy often took their
side. Other than a frequently absent mother,
Tracy had grown up on her own. The noise
and busyness in our house was a welcome
change for her and she enjoyed it. She had
come back to Preston out of choice. I came
back because it was one of the only decent
places I could get a job in my chosen field of
social work. There had been government
cutbacks, and while I would have preferred
to work in Edmonton, Calgary, Red Deer or
any of the larger Canadian cities, Preston was
a good option. Besides, I could live at home
cheaply, which helped me pay off my student
loans and get a decent savings account, aka
"escape" account, started.

"Chip. Hands down or up in the air while
he's flexing his lateral deltoids." I sighed.

"And don't I sound like I know too much about that."

I handed the cashier my debit card and gave the groceries a once-over, making sure I didn't miss any vital items such as chocolate-covered peanuts, pop or something equally nutritious.

"So what did Chip do to earn this attack?"

Where to start, where to start?

"Let me set the stage," I said, watching the cashier bag the trans-fat-loaded food. "It's Monday, which means a cranky supervisor, cranky foster parents and cranky foster kids who've had two more days worth of complaints to heap on my head. On top of that I had one deranged biological father threatening me with a lawsuit if I didn't return his children to him the minute he steps out of jail. I come home tired and ready for a cup of tea and a smidgen of sympathy. I step onto the porch and stumble over Chip's roping saddle parked square in front of the door. As I dance around it, I end up tangled up in a set of reins and fall in a most ungraceful heap on Chip's greasy coveralls. End result—a cleaning bill, bruised hip and a broken heel on the new boots that you and I spent an hour and a half looking for in West Edmonton Mall. So you have a stake in my misery, as well, considering all the grumbling you did on the two-hour drive back from said mall."

I could see from the faint twitch of Tracy's lips that while as a friend and fellow woman she felt sorry for me, as a normal human being with a dose of guy genes herself she could picture my ungainly fall and see the humor in it. I don't think she cared about the boots.

"But you're okay, right?"

My too-deep-for-words sigh told her that she had taken the wrong tack. So she did what any wise friend would do. Change the subject.

"So…moving on to the more mundane things in your life. What are you doing the rest of this afternoon?" Tracy asked as she put her own groceries on the conveyor belt. I glanced at the fresh lettuce, cucumbers, green peppers and fruit and suffered a moment of grocery envy. Tracy's husband, a "man" in my estimation, didn't think that eating salad would diminish his manhood and gladly ate the occasional meatless meal without thinking that he would faint when he left the table.

"After bringing you to the garage, picking up my dry cleaning, getting my shoe repaired and dropping my flat tire off at my brother's shop?" I asked, trying for one last bid of sympathy.

"Yeah."

Well that was dead in the water. "I have to head back to the office to give the other 'guy' in my life, my beloved supervisor, Casey Braeshears, a few moments of my time." I gathered up the super-size-me groceries and swung the last bag into the cart, taking my frustrations out on Neil's nacho chips. Hardly the gourmet food I preferred, but my culinary tastes were vastly outnumbered.

"Forget to paper clip your invoices again?" Tracy asked, in mock horror.

"I'm thinking it's something worse, like letting that teenager I had to drag home from a party borrow a government-issued pen without making him return it." I gave her a resigned look. "The budget, you know, doesn't cover these major, unforeseen expenses."

"You need a new job." Tracy shook her head in sympathy as she waited for her groceries to get bagged.

"Don't I know it. If I could trust my brothers to take care of Dad, I would be heading to the city so fast you wouldn't even see the blink of my taillights."

"I can't believe you would do that. Besides me, what is in the big city that isn't in Preston?" Tracy asked pretending innocence.

"Men. Lots of men and no Casey Braeshears."

"C'mon. I think you could find a few 'men' scattered through Preston if you looked hard enough."

My eye was drawn to the neon yellow of a reflector strip glinting back at me from a hard hat on a man behind Tracy.

His grease-stained plaid jacket, torn blue jeans and work boots showed clearly that this was a working man. He wore sunglasses that hid his eyes, and in spite of his full beard and mustache, I easily caught the smirk on his mouth, the arrogant tilt of his head that showed this working man was also a full-fledged guy.

That and the rolled up motorcycle magazine that he tapped impatiently against his thigh.

Then he lowered his sunglasses enough so I caught a glimpse of bloodshot eyes, and incredibly, he gave me a slow wink.

I gave him my best *so*-not-interested look, then turned my attention back to Tracy.

"Preston is *guy-haven*," I grumbled, raising my voice for the benefit of the guy dropping his magazine in front of the cashier. "There's not a decent single *man* to be found anywhere in this town. I've lost faith in the whole 'seek and ye shall find' concept," I said as Tracy loaded her groceries into my cart.

"You haven't had much of a chance to exercise that faith with the hours you've been working the past year," Tracy protested as she started pushing the cart toward the exit.

In spite of my momentary pique with the guy now at the till, I couldn't help a glance his way, surprised to see him looking directly at me. Or so it seemed from the direction of his sunglasses.

What was worse, he was smirking, as if he had expected me to give him a second look.

I turned away, flustered, then angry at myself.

The electric doors of the supermarket swooshed open ahead of us. "Since Rodney, when was the last time you were on a date?" Tracy was asking.

I pulled my attention back to her. "Does sitting beside Dr. Hardy in church count?"

Tracy ran her fingers through her short dark hair and angled me an exasperated look. "Danielle, the man is sixty."

"He's single," I offered. "Of course, I don't know why I'm fussing about not having a man in my life. I wouldn't have the time for the proper care and maintenance of a relationship if I did."

"You need to let Casey know that you're not a machine," Tracy continued, ignoring my feeble attempt at humor. "That you can't keep working these obscene hours. None of the other social workers in the department do."

"It's not just Casey. My dad and brothers seem to think that supper simply appears out of thin air every day. The boys are even childish enough to believe in the laundry fairy, who comes and does their clothes every day."

"You should get them to help more."

"I should also try to bring about world peace and reconcile every broken home."

"You are working on the last part."

"I might have a better chance at a city job if I can show how invaluable I am here." I grabbed the handle of the cart and started traversing the parking lot.

"Why not tell Casey to hire another social worker?"

"Like that's going to happen. He's got to submit his budget for the next fiscal year and he's squeezing water out of pennies to maintain his cheapskate status. It's a status any normal person would be ashamed to admit to, but Casey is convinced it is going to get him career tenure in social services. I wonder if he gets frequent flier miles for every penny he saves the department." We rattled our way to my waiting car, the sun shining benevolently down on us. It was spring in the country and usually the lengthening days and the increasing warmth brought out joy and happiness in me. But work had kept me too busy to take time to appreciate the freshness of the air and the unfurling of new green leaves.

Tracy's car was getting an oil change and she had needed a ride from work to the grocery store, so I quit work a half hour early to help her out. Casey must have gotten wind of my defection, and this little meeting was his way of wringing out every possible minute of work from me. I paused, wondering when and how I should tell her.

I took a deep breath and then I took the plunge.

"You may as well know I'm looking at another job." I rattled out the words faster than the wobble on my grocery cart. "It's regular hours, and I'll be reporting to a normal boss."

"Good for you. It's about time. Who is this for?"

"It's for a private adoption agency." I waited a moment, gathering my strength to drop the next bomb. "It's in the city. In Edmonton."

I didn't want to see Tracy's face. So I rattled on, keeping my eyes on my trusty Civic, circa 1989 and still going strong, thanks to Chip's mechanical abilities and body filler, courtesy of Neil. My brothers had their good points.

"But that's a two-hour drive," she wailed

"Depends on who's driving," I offered helpfully. "Chip's done it in one hour ten minutes."

"Chip also has about half a demerit point before the Mounties take his license away for life," Tracy retorted, clearly put out with my breaking news. "You can't go. I need you. Your foster kids need you. Your family needs…your father needs you," she hastily amended.

I sighed. And that was the crux of the matter. Six weeks ago I had started looking around for my own place to live and another job. Then Dad collapsed at the auction mart in Kolvik and everything changed.

All my life, Dad had been the epitome of strong faith and good humor. Even after our mother, Alice, died a number of years ago, he had grieved hard, then told us all he put his trust in God and went back to being the fun-loving, encouraging man he was. But after the heart attack he had become weak and frail and given to bouts of deep depression. These days he didn't even have the strength or the will to get up from his recliner or to crack open the Bible that he had read every day for as long as I could remember. My brothers, who stopped going to church when my mom died, didn't share my concerns. Reading the Bible did not seem to be on the "approved" list of activities for guys.

I couldn't leave my father this way, but I had stayed as long as I could.

"I'm not moving to New Zealand." I pulled open the back door of my car.

"I don't drive like Chip so it would be a four-hour round trip." Tracy set her bags in the back and slammed the door shut. "That's a lot of time to spend in a vehicle just for the pleasure of your company."

"I would come home most weekends," I said, still loading up my own groceries. A week's supply of healthy food obviously took less time to load than three days' worth of junk food. "I have enough reasons to come back to Preston."

Tracy didn't reply as we got into the car. She didn't say anything as I reversed out of my spot and turned onto the street. She didn't say anything when we headed toward the garage where they were working on her car. She didn't say anything as I pulled into the customer parking stall.

It was her turn to talk, but as I put my car into Park I gave in. "Tracy, you said yourself that I needed to get another job. I heard you."

"I said you needed to talk to your boss about your job. Not…not…" She spun her hand in a circle, wiping away what I had told her. "This moving thing you want to do. That you didn't even talk about with me. That you couldn't even bother to ask me questions about even though you knew I would be as upset as I am now." Tracy complained in a voice that conveyed to me her utter disbelief that I would seriously want to leave home and community and head to the big, bad city.

I tried to find the words that would make her understand, as I wrapped my hands around the steering wheel and rested my chin on it, staring through the window of the garage in front of us. "You see that man?" I asked Tracy, lifting my pinky finger to point at Tom Grady. "He pulled me out of Frieson's pond when my brothers dared me to skate across it. He told me to be quiet in church when I was a crazy teenager sitting with her friends. He loves to tease me about an especially touching moment of the Christmas program when I, as an innocent girl of five, lifted up the skirt of my best Sunday dress as I stood on the stage displaying my underwear to my horrified family members and an amused public. There are at least a dozen people who have some kind of memory of me that is either unflattering or embarrassing. There are no secrets in this town for me. There is no mystery. No surprises."

"I can see why you want to leave. Sort of," Tracy conceded. "But I'm selfish. And I want you here. With me and David."

"I know. And I love you and David, too. But with me and my brothers, well, I'm losing the love. They're turning into permanent residents. If I want to be released from guy-dom, I have to move out."

"But the city…"

I don't know why I had hoped she would support my decision. Tracy was warming to hearth and home of late. She had even bought David a pair of slippers. Next was an SUV and the requisite Labrador retriever. From there it was a quick slip into having children, and I knew she wanted to share each step with me. The way my love life was unfolding, I wasn't going to catch up any time soon.

"It might not happen," I said with a lame attempt at reconciliation. "I could spend the rest of my days stuck here in town with Dad and the boys and their toys and dirt and stuff, turning into an old maid who reminisces about the few dates she went on with the occasional man that made Preston a momentary stopping point in his climb up the career ladder."

"I can see that I'm not going to get anywhere with you today," Tracy said primly, pushing open the door. "I'll go see if my car is ready."

Tracy disappeared into the building, the tilt of her dark head telling me more than her parting comment did. The vibration of my cell phone gave me something else to think about. The number gave me something else to sigh about. It was my brother Neil.

"Hey, babe," he said as I flipped open the phone and mumbled hello. "Can you stop by the shop? Chip needs a ride home to pick up my truck and bring it here."

"I was going to come anyway to get you guys to fix my flat tire," I said, glancing quickly at my watch. Neil and Chip worked at another mechanic's shop in town and I liked to give them my business. Tracy's husband David got all his mechanic work at Grady's. When they got married, Tracy started going there, too. I thought this took the whole "whither thou goest I will go" part of the wedding vows they exchanged too far. As for me, I went to the place my brothers worked at because I often got a deal on work done on my car. "But first I have to stop at the office then run a couple of errands."

"So?"

"So that means he'll have to wait for about an hour."

"Hang on a sec, I'll tell him." He put the phone down. Over the clanging of metal I could hear Neil deliver this information to my other brother, then some muttered conversation, followed by a shouted-out greeting to someone entering the shop. Then a burst of laughter. Sounded like they were having fun. I waited and waited. No surprise that their time was more valuable than mine.

I heard the low murmur of conversation and then another burst of laughter. Neil picked up the phone again. "You comin' right away after that, though? It's okay with Chip."

Be still my heart.

Tracy poked her head out of the door and gave me a thumbs-up to indicate that her car was ready.

"I'll be there as soon as I'm done," I muttered as I got out of my car to help Tracy bring her groceries to hers.

I snapped the phone shut, grabbed a couple of bags out of the car and brought them around the side of the building where her car was parked. She closed the door on the groceries in the backseat, then waited a moment as if she wanted to say something more to me.

I knew I had thrown out the information about my move without much preparation, but at the same time I didn't know a better way to tell her. Between working with kids whose first language was not found in any respectable dictionary and brothers who thought tact was something you used to spear notices to the wall, my diplomacy was worn thin.

"Well, I don't want to keep Casey waiting." I waited another beat, then, as I turned to leave, Tracy caught me by the arm.

"I'm sorry. I'm feeling a little pouty right now." She gave me an apologetic smile. "I had visions of me and David and you and Someone Special growing up in Preston together and sharing recipes and swapping babysitting and all those kind of things that you see in life insurance commercials."

I knew full well what Tracy had grown up with and how she longed for a life that at least veered toward normal territory. And I knew she wanted me to be a part of that.

"Hey, you never know. Maybe I'll meet the perfect man and he'll want to move to Preston...."

"And maybe your brothers will buy you red roses," Tracy put in, referring to an ongoing joke.

"It could happen."

"I don't want to think about you going yet. For now, I'm going to go home, unload my groceries and then sit down and start praying."

"No fair," I protested. "I have to do all my

praying on the run. There's no way I can compete with you."

"It's not a competition," Tracy said.

"Well, I know what you'll be praying for," I muttered. "For me to stay here."

"You're just guessing at that." She grew serious and laid a hand on my arm. "I always pray for you, Danielle. I pray that God will keep you safe. I pray that you will find strength to do your job. Now I have to add that you'll find someone here in Preston to love."

"That's unlikely," I said.

"Well, you make sure you get your brothers to help you unload that tire."

I laughed. "That would never happen. My brothers haven't spent all those years teaching me to be self-sufficient only to jump in at this time of my life."

Tracy shook her head. "Someday, some woman is going to have one of those guys on the run. Mark my words."

"I will. And I'll be there with pom-poms cheering her on." I punched the air, underlining my comment.

Thankfully the meeting with Casey turned into his usual petty whine about me taking too much overtime and how I should learn to prioritize. I pulled out my "understanding" expression, listened dutifully for twenty minutes while I twisted my hands in my lap so I wouldn't be tempted to hit him. Striking your boss does not look good on a resume especially if he's the only reference you have. With Casey I had to tread extra carefully since I told him I was looking for other work. I had to make sure he had no reason to get petty. Soon I was back in my car headed back downtown. At the dry cleaner's, I chatted with an old friend and made the appropriate admiring noises when she showed me her engagement ring. I knew the guy she was marrying, so jealousy wasn't an issue, but being reminded of my own single status was. I knew in this day and age I should be embracing my independence, but truthfully, I'd sooner be embracing a man.

Next stop was the shoe store to pick up my now fixed boot and endure a lecture on how to polish them so this expensive footwear would last longer. Then, I finally pulled up to the mechanic's garage where Chip and Neil worked.

The front door was locked, but I knew from past experience that the side door would be open. I parked beside an unfamiliar truck with an unfamiliar logo, whipped that tire out of the trunk of my car with an expert twist of my hips and kept my skirt clean.

I was good.

Tracy's comment about getting the boys to help made me laugh. They would say they were busy; they would ask me if my arms were broken, I was tough. I'm sure there were times they thought the skirts and dresses I wore were clever disguises to fool them into thinking I might actually be different from them.

The flat tire was hard to roll, but once I got it going, it went okay. The door was tricky and from the sounds of laughter inside, I guessed the truck belonged to a long lost buddy of one of my brothers.

Yay. Just what I needed in my current mood. Another guy.

And wasn't it simply divine justice that the guy perched on the bumper of Chip's truck was the same "guy" I had seen in the grocery store still wearing his sunglasses.

"And out of nowhere comes the sunshine," he announced, watching me as I manhandled the tire toward the tire changer, but making no move to help. Did these guys think rolling flat tires qualified as a spectator sport?

"Pretty little lady is pretty tough," he said, angling me another smile.

He had to be kidding. Sunshine? Pretty little lady? Could this guy get any more guyish? I ignored him this time.

Chip wiped his hands on a greasy towel and watched me. Neil finally grabbed the tire. Jace leaned against the truck, grinning at their new friend as if he had said something wildly original.

"Hey, sis. You're late," Jace called out as Neil dropped the tire by the compressor.

"Hey, Jace. I don't care," I retorted, not bothering to pull out my manners. Even though Tracy and I had made up, I still felt grumbly. This guy's unsubtle come-on as he watched me struggle, piled on top of Casey's earlier patronizing attitude, didn't help to push my mood out of the red zone.

"Okay if I bring this back later on?" Neil asked.

"I can make it home on the spare."

"Jigs, this is our sister Danielle," Chip said as he tossed the towel into a nearby can. "Jigs likes fishing."

I presumed this was Chip's way of explaining how he had come up with this particular nickname. Chip only re-christened guys he considered good friends. Jigs obviously made a huge impression very quickly. I'd heard vague references to Jigs in the past few days but I'd been too busy to follow through. And definitely not interested.

I gave him a careful smile accompanied by what my brothers called my office telephone voice. "Welcome to Preston," I said, pleased that I sounded so civil.

"Thanks for that," he said, tipping his hard hat back on his head and grinning at me again. "Preston seems like a real friendly town."

I gave him a vague look.

"I'm thinking of moving here," he continued, obviously oblivious to my not-interested attitude. "I've heard good things about this place and—" he paused and grinned at me "—the people in it."

"Isn't that great?" Jace said, looking as if his favorite dog had just come home.

"Wonderful," I murmured, ignoring the vague innuendo in Jigs's comment. Duty done, I turned back to Chip. "You ready to go?"

Chip glanced from me to Jigs, then to Jace, his expression clearly puzzled.

I lifted my eyebrow in question and resisted the urge to tap my foot.

I saw Jace shrug, then slowly shake his head in surprise.

I wasn't stupid. I read in their unsubtle body language that I hadn't done something I was supposed to.

Then I saw Neil poke Jace in the side and give him the taunting grin of winner to loser. "Told you she was fussy," I heard him whisper.

"That's okay," Jace said with a grin overflowing with masculine self-confidence. "She'll come around."

Chapter Two

As I looked at the expectant faces of my brothers and Jigs's smug expression, realization dawned in Technicolor.

I was supposed to have fallen for the obvious charms of this Jigs guy, thereby making my brothers the happiest men in the world. I couldn't believe these guys. They were a testosterone-laden version of The Little Engine That Could. They didn't quit.

A month ago they introduced me to a heavy-duty mechanic who was, they claimed, sensitive because he owned two black Labs that rode around with him in the cab of his pickup. Two weeks before that, it was a guy who worked for the department of highways and did extreme mountain biking in his spare time. Before that it was some cowboy who was always on the road but was in the top ten in the Wild Rose Rodeo Association—like that was enough to make me fall head over heels in love with him.

My brothers lived in mortal fear that I would end up marrying someone who could talk for over five minutes and not bring up internal combustion engines, the fate of certain hockey teams, the price of feed wheat or anything to do with horses.

I suspected this Jigs guy was their latest effort at the game, but with their usual ineptness, once again they missed the matchmaking mark.

I gave Jace my vintage ticked-off-sister look—the kind reserved for moments when my brothers had gone over their quota of silliness.

Jace had the grace to look somewhat abashed. Chip was looking at me, as if he expected me to throw myself into this bushman's arms and declare undying love. Neil just looked interested.

Jigs, however, had a curious half smirk on his face, as if he saw me as a prize that, given time, would be his. That annoyed me most of all.

As I stalked out of the garage I heard Neil say, "I'll bet you any money, she'll change her mind."

"You're on," I heard Chip cry out.

Brothers, I thought dismissively. Guys one and all.

I started my car again and waited for Chip to join me. I closed my eyes, laid my head back against the headrest of my car and prayed for patience. And whatever else I would need. I loved my brothers but they had to stop thinking that all they had to do was parade what they thought was a suitable guy in front of me and I would fall for him like a roped calf.

The car door opened and Chip jumped in. "Sorry to make you wait. I had to… uh…answer the phone. Business stuff." He gave me his best sweet-little-boy smile, pretending that awkward moment in the garage hadn't happened.

"Chip? This guy, Jigs? Not such a good idea. You're going to lose your bet."

"You haven't even given him a chance," he sputtered. "Jigs is a great guy. He loves to play hockey, he likes fishing and even did a few circuits of the rodeo a couple of years ago."

Chip didn't even seem to realize that all of these so-called good points were severely impairing their friend's appeal quotient.

"He thinks you're cute," Chip added. This, of course, sealed the deal. How could I *not* fall for a guy who thought I was "cute."

"He hasn't even met me," I said, pretending to forget that I had seen him in the store.

"He saw your picture on the wall."

In spite of my frustration with my brothers from time to time, I knew they loved me. How many guys would hang a picture of their sister up alongside the requisite calendar girls in the place they worked?

"He's a great guy," Chip said, clearly campaigning for his friend.

"I'm sure as far as you guys are concerned, he fits right in," I agreed, hence my hesitation. "But I'm not interested. Besides, if I get this job in Edmonton, I won't be around anyway."

Chip tapped his fingers on his leg. "Why do you want to go, anyway?"

I had gone over this ground so many times it was dust. "I've told you enough times, Chip. I want to get out of Preston. I want to meet new people. I want to run away and join a different circus."

"You just hope to connect with some lawyer or accountant or some guy who goes to work in a suit."

"You make that sound like a disease," I said turning my car onto Preston's main road.

"It's unnatural, is what it is," Chip grumped. "You're going to end up with some guy who uses words like 'actualize' and 'agenda' and we're going to end up looking like a bunch of dumb farm hicks."

"You're being prejudiced. There's lots of nice men out there," I said, knowing partially where his anger came from.

Because of his dyslexia, Chip had struggled through his classes until he got to high school. There he enrolled in a good vocational program where he excelled in mechanics. Chip had always helped my dad and brothers fix the machinery on the farm and he had a surprising connection with engines. He parlayed that into an apprenticeship and as soon as he got his journeyman's ticket at a tech school in Edmonton, he had come back to Preston to work at the same garage Neil worked at.

He had done well for himself, but along the way his self-esteem had taken a few blows from those who had done better in school.

He'd had a dream of starting his own business with Neil, but when he'd gone to a bank to apply for a loan, he'd been treated poorly by one of the loan officers there, an old schoolmate. A man in a suit who used words like "agenda" and "actualize."

My other brothers' own disregard for professional men didn't have the same deep-seated angst. They plain didn't like men who they couldn't relate to.

"You're only as dumb as you let people think you are," I said, letting a touch of anger slip into my voice. "And if you were serious about starting your own business, you wouldn't let one petty loan officer scare you away. There are other banks and other people you can deal with."

A stubborn silence met that remark, and I backed off. Chip was immovable once he'd made up his mind.

"And how was work today?" I asked, shifting back into sister mode.

"Busy. Old man Thompkins brought his tractor in. A gear in the tranny piled up. Then one of Brody Cherwonka's guys brought his buncher in and it's going to need a final drive. We're swamped."

Chip delivered this information like I should know what a final drive was and that I knew Mr. Thompkins would need a new transmission.

The trouble was, I did.

For a woman who liked pastel colors, manicures, gourmet food, classical music and good books, I knew far too much about mechanics, farming, welding, hockey and rodeo.

"What time are you guys going to be home?" I asked as I turned the car into the driveway of the farm.

"Not for another hour, maybe more," Chip said. "I got to bring Neil's truck back and maybe have a quick look at it to see if I need to order any parts."

I knew from past experience that Chip's "quick look" meant that I wouldn't be done with the dishes until nine o'clock.

As we got closer to the house I saw smoke pluming out of the chimney. My mood lifted. Dad had obviously been feeling well enough to start a fire in the fireplace, which meant the house would be toasty warm. I longed for a cup of hot tea and a moment to sit and relax in front of a snapping fire before I started making supper. If Dad was in a good mood, I would at least have a few hours to read.

Chip got into Neil's truck as I parked my car and hurried to the house, to enjoy the warmth and the company of my father.

It was late afternoon the next day and the restaurant of the Preston Inn held only a smattering of people, most of whom I recognized. Wednesday at the inn was usually a quiet affair.

Tracy had called me before I left, apologizing for the fact that she wouldn't be able to meet me for our biweekly supper date. One of David's clients had cancelled, which left David free. Then Tracy's mother had called and unexpectedly asked her and David to come for supper.

Tracy had only recently reconciled with her estranged mother so I encouraged her to take Velma up on the offer.

That left me dateless, and I didn't feel like going home to cook for my brothers.

"Are you waiting for Tracy?" Jessica, one of the regular waitresses at the inn, asked me.

I shook my head, trying not to feel sorry for myself. I was getting really good at it, but even though practice makes perfect there were some skills that didn't look good on a resume. "She couldn't come. So I'm on my own."

"Too bad. Well, just go sit down, and I'll be right there," Jessica said and hurried toward the kitchen.

I wandered over to Tracy's and my usual spot. When Jessica came, I ordered my usual cup of Earl Grey tea and my usual chicken breast entrée, and glanced out the usual window at the unchanging face of Preston. Across from the inn a few cows had their heads buried in a feeder. The rest of the Samson herd was huddled in the shelter of a wind-fence that Donald Samson had put up two summers ago. I knew that because Tracy and I had watched the progress from these very seats by this very window.

As I waited for my dinner, sipping my tea, I reminded myself that sitting by myself would be good practice for when I moved to the city. I would have to get used to being on my own until I established a network of friends.

I felt a moment of panic. In spite of my big-city pretensions, I couldn't hide the fact that I was born and raised in the country. Would I be an obvious hick? I didn't know what a Hermès scarf looked like and had no clue about Prada or Chloe or any other designers. I was strictly a Sheiling Boutique and Arth's

Fashion Centre kind of girl. Wasn't a city girl supposed to aspire to this kind of knowledge?

A movement on my right side caught my attention and drew me back to the land of the normal. Well, Preston normal.

A tall man sat down at the table beside me, taking a seat on the opposite side and giving me a clear look at him. His well-cut suit emphasized the breadth of his shoulders, its soft grey setting off his light brown hair with its faint wave. His hazel eyes were fringed with thick, dark lashes that made me jealous. Well-defined nose, firm mouth. Faint hint of a five-o'clock shadow but not enough to make him look scruffy.

He didn't look familiar but he certainly looked good. He looked like the kind of man my brothers would immediately distrust.

He glanced up in time to catch me staring at him. When he smiled I blushed and looked away.

This was not being responsible, I told myself. He's a complete stranger. Didn't your mother always tell you…

But then another man stopped by his table. It was Eric Lougheed, the manager of one of the banks in town. Eric was as straightlaced as a Victorian grandma. He glanced at me, gave me a vague nod, then turned back to my mystery man. I tried to listen and tried to look as if I weren't listening, but in spite of my nonchalance, I still didn't catch the handsome stranger's name. Either Eric and he weren't on a first-name basis or they knew each other so well, they didn't have to exchange names.

After Eric left, I waited a suitable moment, then let my eyes wander oh-so-casually around the restaurant, drifting past the stranger, then stopping when I saw that he was reading a book. I couldn't see the title, but I could see that it was fiction. Huge points here. The only book my brothers read were the Truck and Heavy Equipment Traders or parts books.

After a few minutes, he glanced up at me and smiled again. As if he knew me. "Hello, Danielle. How are you?" he asked, his voice deep, with a hint of roughness.

He knew who I was. But who was he?

Client? Lawyer I had met during one of my cases? Department person? Social worker? Salesman?

Out of habit I glanced at his left hand. No

ring, so not married. Eric knew him so that ruled out potential axe murderer.

"I'm fine," I said, holding his gaze as my mind raced, feeling dumber the longer he looked at me. Maybe I'd remember his name if I kept him talking. "And you? How are you?" Oh, very intelligent repartee. "Are you here on business?"

He nodded.

Just then Jessica came between us carrying my supper. I thanked her for the food then waited for her to go so I could try to remember this good-looking man.

"So how are Tracy and David doing?" Jessica asked, lingering a moment. "I think it's so cool that they are building their own house."

Usually I didn't mind a bit of conversation. Usually I was glad to talk about Tracy and David, my good friends, and their happiness and how things have worked out so well for Tracy.

But right now all I wanted was for Jessica to leave so I could chat with the mysterious but good-looking man sitting a few feet away from me who knew who I was.

I am a pathetic and sad creature, but I figured I was due for a good look at a real live man after the little Jigs deal the other day. So I gave concise, noncommittal answers until Jessica left and I was alone.

And the very good-looking maybe-single man was still sitting at his table, still looking at me.

I usually prayed before my meal. But this man was watching. Would he figure I was a fanatic who was going to push tracts at him while he ate and ask him if he had a personal relationship with Jesus?

He who honors Me I will honor him. The words from Samuel gently settled in my head and I realized that I was quickly splashing toward the shallow end of my gene pool.

So I sent up an apology, bowed my head and tried to concentrate on my prayer. It took a bit, but I slowly worked my way toward sincerity and when I was done, gentle peace suffused through me. I was thankful God understood and forgave. And He knew my constant need of both.

I looked up to see the man watching me with a whimsical expression on his face.

"I'm sorry for staring," he said quietly. "It's not often you see someone praying in public. I think that's wonderful."

"Thank you." Did he go to church, too? Could I be so fortunate as to meet not only a man, but a Christian one? "It's not a big thing."

"Maybe not to you, but I think it's admirable." He put his book down and picked up the menu. "So, Danielle, is there anything on the menu that you recommend?"

There he was with the name again. This was driving me crazy. Why could I not remember who he was? College? Had to be.

"The chicken is good if you want an entrée and so are the ribs, but they're a little messy." High school? One of those geeky types who one day morph into Mr. Irresistible? "I personally recommend the pecan pie." Had to be high school. He reminded me of Ron Dessler, my Grade 10 chem partner.

"I think I'll have the chicken." He set the menu on one corner of the table, eased the knot of his tie and undid the top button.

Okay, I'm a weak woman but there's something vaguely intimate about a man loosening his tie. I get the same little thrill when I see a man unbutton his cuffs and roll up the sleeves.

And I knew that I had to find out who this man was. "I'm sorry, but I have to confess that I can't remember your name. Forgive me."

He slowly released a devastating smile and held my gaze. "My name is James. James Ashby."

Nope. Still not ringing any bells.

He angled his head toward the empty seat across from me. "Do you mind if I join you?"

"No. Please do. Eating alone does have the tendency to make one look like a loser, doesn't it?" Too late, I realized what I had said. "Not that I'm implying you're a…well…"

"Of course you're not," he said with a light laugh as he got up. I didn't realize how tall he was until he sat directly across from me, his elbows resting on the table, his hazel eyes holding a hint of humor and a few very attractive flecks of gold.

"I usually have better manners," I said, pushing my potatoes around on my plate with my fork. "Living with three brothers, who are full-fledged guys, has taken the edge off my social graces."

"Guys. What do you mean by that?" James asked.

"You see, there are two types of males in the world," I explained. "Guys and men."

"The difference being?"

"Very simple. If a man comes across a beautiful, quiet canyon, he will take a picture of it. A guy will belch to see if he can get an echo. A man will give you the shirt off his back, a guy will give you a piece of his mind. A man will campaign for world peace, a guy will campaign for peace between NHL players and the owners. My brothers are guys."

"And that's bad because…?" James asked.

"It's not bad. In the whole issue of guy-dom, women and women's needs aren't as important as risking your neck."

"I see. And you've done extensive studies on this?" I could hear the amusement in his voice.

"A lifetime of experience," I said. "I grew up hiding my Barbie dolls under the bed so my brothers couldn't put them in their homemade rockets and launch them into the nearest pond. I'd have to make sure they didn't get hold of my hair-spray pump so they could put food coloring in it. I spent half my teen years finding hiding spots for my diary so I wouldn't have to listen to them reading it out loud to their friends."

I caught a glimmer of a smile on James's face. "I can see that your life has been difficult," he said.

"Not difficult. Just challenging." Time to

turn the conversation around. "What about you, James? Any family?"

"One sister. She's nineteen and she is a challenge, but of the female sort. She used to live with my aunt and uncle but she moved out as soon as she could. I get the occasional call on my cell phone, but otherwise I don't hear much from her."

"No parents?"

James shook his head, then smiled at Jessica when she brought his dinner. She gave me a meaningful look, then, thankfully, left.

"And how is your father doing?" he asked, as he unwrapped his cutlery from the paper napkin. "I understand he had a heart attack?"

"Thanks for asking. He's doing okay. Listless, though. I've been trying to take care of him."

"He's lucky to have such a loving daughter."

"I do love him," I said with a light shrug. "And I love my brothers. I just wish they would let me carry on with my life without so much interference."

"Now how could a brother interfere with your life? I've been trying to do the same with my sister without any success."

So I told him about some of the "guys" my

brothers have brought around. He laughed in sympathy and told me about some of the "guys" his sister had dated. I discovered that he was worried about her and how protective he'd been when they were growing up. Our conversation wound down after a while and I allowed myself a faint glow of anticipation.

James finished his supper, wiped his mouth with a napkin and sat back, smiling at me. "Besides the occasional movie, is there anything exciting going on in this town in the next week?"

"Tomorrow night the bakery is having a special on raisin buns," I offered.

His half smile increased the pace of my heart. "I was hoping to ask you to accompany me on some kind of outing, but somehow raisin buns weren't in my fantasy."

Outing. Was that the same as a date?

"But I would be willing to settle for a movie tomorrow, if you are." His dark brown voice washed over me like rich chocolate.

I would say that movie equals date. "I think I could be satisfied with that," I said, not sounding very suave or sophisticated. But I felt kind of happy in spite of my lack thereof.

His smile bloomed, making the corners of

his eyes crinkle in a decidedly appealing manner. "That sounds good to me. Let me know where you live and I can pick you up."

"No. I can't do that."

Chapter Three

"Pardon me?" he asked, clearly confused.

"No. I'd like to go with you to the movie," I amended hastily. "But it would be better if I meet you there. I live quite a ways away and it's gravel roads and if you have a car it's kind of hard on the car and besides, I don't give good directions."

Stop. Stop.

I took a breath and hoped that my sudden babbling wouldn't convince him I was a complete idiot. I was trying to stave off imminent disaster. If my brothers met him and he wore anything resembling the suit or a tie he had on today, they would ask him embarrassing questions and make him feel like a geek and he would get scared off. Or worse yet, they would bring that hairy Jigs guy over again as an antidote so he could wink at me and make more strange comments and watch me work. No thanks.

"I would prefer to come pick you up," he insisted.

"No. Let's keep things casual," I said breezily, trying to make up lost ground. After all, I still didn't really know who he was. Only that he was kind, considerate and had a younger sister that he cared about.

Which raised his suitability quotient to "very."

"I'll meet you there."

He gave me a slow-release smile that made my heart dance. "Okay. It's a date."

"A date? Are you sure? Don't you want to run a background check on him?" Tracy's question on the other end of the phone raised a few alarms again, but I thought of how James had smiled at me when he saw me praying. "He claims to know you, but if you don't know or remember him, shouldn't you be concerned? Shouldn't you be thinking 'stalker'?"

I didn't like how Tracy's questions brought

out those niggling doubts about the first date I've had with a halfway decent man in this town for the past few years.

"The only stalker I need to worry about is Steve Stinson and he's been laying low," I said, adjusting my headset as I signed off on a set of forms. Steve Stinson was the biological father of Kent, a little boy we had in our care. Though I wasn't Kent's caseworker, I had been initially involved when Tracy brought Kent's neglected state to my attention. In Steve's twisted mind, I was the person responsible for keeping him away from Kent. So I was the lucky recipient of his phone calls. "Besides, Eric knows James."

"Eric is mean to his cats," Tracy said. As a vet tech she got to see firsthand how people treated their pets and as far as Tracy was concerned, anyone who was mean to their pets wasn't worth knowing, and by extension, neither were the people they associated with.

"That doesn't mean that James is," I said, doodling the letter "J" on my notepad. "He seems like a perfectly respectable citizen."

"Where does he live?"

"He said he's looking at a place on the outskirts of town."

"Wow. That makes things crystal clear."

I stifled a sigh. Tracy was getting as protective as my brothers. I hadn't told them about this date. As far as I was concerned, they were on a "need to know" basis and this they didn't need to know. For a *long* time. Maybe never. Well, maybe I'd invite them to the wedding. They could be ushers.

"I think I can spot sincerity when I see it," I said. Bobby, my secretary, tapped on my door and handed me a sheaf of phone messages that she had taken while I was at a case conference earlier that day. I groaned when I saw the thick stack.

"But the most crafty psychopaths are the ones that present a normal personality at first," Tracy said.

"I'm not calling off the date and he's not a psychopath."

"I wouldn't mind meeting him so I can see for myself."

"Tracy, you're getting as bad as my brothers." I was starting to feel angry. "He's a nice guy. He's good-looking. He wears a suit and he reads books that have chapters and no pictures. I wish you would trust my judgment."

"Sorry. I don't want to see you hurt."

"It's just a date. What's to hurt?"

Tracy sighed lightly. "Your heart. I know what a romantic you are."

"You should be happy about this, Tracy. If he turns out to be a caring, sensitive man, I might end up sticking around," I said, sorting the messages into important, very important and panic.

"Don' tell me you're dating him so you can make me happy."

"Actually, Tracy, I'm not that self-sacrificial...." My voice trailed off as the name on one of the messages caught my attention. Steve Stinson.

"What's wrong?"

"Nothing. Hey, I gotta go. But just to reassure you, I won't elope with him without consulting you first."

"Thanks, hon," Tracy said dryly. "Nice to know you'll keep me in the loop. But just to be on the safe side I'm going to do an Internet search of his name."

We said goodbye and as I disconnected I let myself heave a sigh. I *so* did not want to talk to Steve Stinson. He not only made me angry, he gave me the creeps.

But if I didn't talk to him, he was going to

be hassling Emily and Adam, Kent's foster parents. I usually passed him on to Oden, Kent's caseworker, but Steve wasn't clueing in to the fact that I could not help him. So it was just easier to deal with him myself.

Kent had been placed in Emily and Adam's home when his natural mother, Juanita, ended up in the hospital courtesy of Steve Stinson. Juanita was trying to get her life back together and so far, it looked as if she were succeeding. Juanita had grown up with her own difficulties, but thanks to Emily and Adam, she was learning good parenting and life skills. In a few months we were going to be reassessing her situation. As long as Steve, who claimed to be Kent's natural father, stayed out of the picture, she had a chance at a new life.

I put his message to one side and decided to deal with some of the more pleasant phone calls, such as Andrew Newton, who used curse words as filler when he didn't know what else to say. Pleasant was all a matter of perspective in this job.

"Next time we'll have to do the symphony," James said as he held the door of the movie theater open for me Thursday evening. I had forgotten to check what the movie of the week was. Multiplex and small town are not two words that go together. Consequently my notion of a quiet evening in the intimacy of a darkened movie theater had been chased away by exploding cars and gunshots and a high body count all cheered on by a large contingent of adolescent boys.

"It was okay. I don't mind action movies." I shivered as the spring evening air washed over me.

I unfolded my sweater, which I had been carrying over my arm, and tried to put it on.

"Here, let me help you with that." He was right there, pulling the sweater around my shoulders, his hands lingering a few seconds longer than they had to but not so long that it could be taken as a come-on.

Perfect gentleman. I sighed, wanting to draw out the evening.

"Thanks." I hesitated. My car was parked around the corner. James had come from the other direction. I wasn't ready to end the evening, but my insistence on meeting him at the theater made it difficult to figure out what to do from here.

"Is there anywhere we can go for a cup of coffee or something?" James asked as the shouts of young boys, pumped up by the action of the movie, broke into the moment.

"Not really. Just the bar," I said as a joke.

"Pass."

Better and better. "We could go for a walk. There's a lovely paved trail not far from here that follows the river for a ways."

James tilted me a crooked smile. "That sounds like a good idea." He tucked his hands into his pockets as we walked away from the theater. "And again, I have to apologize for the movie. I was quite sure they were showing that indie film I had been wanting to see."

I knew which movie he was referring to and, to be honest, I preferred the action adventure movie we had just seen. I wasn't big on watching the "dissemination of a relationship within the confines of cultural biases" or something like that.

"Small movies like that only stick around here a day or so, if and when they come," I said. "The owner is a huge fan of indie films and tries to sneak one in from time to time. They don't go over well."

James gave me a puzzled glance. "I'm guessing you're not a fan?"

I lifted my shoulders in a careful shrug. I didn't want him to think I was a complete Philistine but at the same time I knew I had to be honest.

"Sorry. No."

"That surprises me. Your... You seem like the kind of person that would like that type of film."

"I've enjoyed a few of them, but many seem to be what I would call artistic temper tantrums. An artist indulging his whims through the medium of film." I chose my words carefully. "I think art should serve the community, not be a vehicle for self-expression." And didn't that sound all cultural and intelligent?

"That's a well-thought-out concept," he said. "But I still think we should go to the symphony next time."

Next time. I liked the sound of those words. I gave James another sidelong glance. He was dressed more casually today. Khaki pants, a V-neck sweater over a shirt. Kind of yuppieish. For a moment I wondered what he would look like in blue jeans.

A light breeze tugged at my hair, but his didn't even budge thanks to the gel that held it firmly in place. I had to fight the temptation to mess it up a little.

I guess I wasn't used to being in the presence of a man so well put together. It seemed a little odd, that was all.

"What kind of music do you like to listen to?" I asked, pulling my sweater around me. He immediately reached around and adjusted it, his movements solicitous. This time he let his hand rest on my shoulder. It was warm and cozy and sent shivers down my spine.

"I'm a fan of Schubert."

"Oh. Why is that?" I thought he would say blues or rock or classical, but Schubert?

"What I appreciate the most about Schubert is his unfolding of long melodies both brusque and leisurely, the blessed earmark of Schubert's style." He gave me an embarrassed smile. "Sorry, I'm a big fan."

"I see that," I said, looking ahead, trying desperately to think of anything positive I could say about my favorite group, Lifehouse. But I was drawing a blank beyond "I like their music." If pushed I could comment on the light notes of grace and redemption I found in their music. I wasn't even going to mention my secret vice, Keith Urban.

"What classical composer do you like the best?" he asked me.

I should have seen this coming. Think. Think. "Bach," I said with a sudden desperation. "I like Bach." I remember taking a course in college where we were told that Bach said he wrote all his music to the glory of God and ever since then I thought he was kind of cool. For a long-dead composer. I liked some of his music. The Hallelujah Chorus.

Or did Handel write that? Think. Think.

"Bach has some very moving pieces," James said, his hand ever so gently pulling me closer as he steered me past a hole in the sidewalk.

I glanced up at him, surprised to find him looking down at me.

Goodness, his eyelashes are almost longer than mine, I thought, letting myself hold his gaze a few seconds longer, moving from friendly into "very interested" territory.

His steps slowed. So did mine.

He stopped, turned toward me. I stopped, facing him. It was quiet down here by the river. Restful. Wind sighed in the trees overhead, water burbled over the rocks.

"You are a beautiful woman," James said, lightly brushing my hair back from my face. "Fair tresses man's imperial race insnare, and beauty draws us with a single hair." Another smile. "Alexander Pope wrote that."

Poetry. My knees went weak as I looked up into his hazel eyes, liking how they crinkled at the corners, as if he were ready to share a joke.

"I'd like to see you again," he said, his fingers lingering in my fair tresses.

"Hey. Hemstead. Don't move. We gotta talk."

The nasal voice of Steve Stinson coming up behind me made me want to scream.

How did he find me? Had he been following me? The thought sent a chill through me.

I braced myself, and turned to face him, glad that I had James beside me. The liquor fumes wafting from Steve's direction made my eyes water.

I hadn't returned Steve's call and the next message I got from him via Bobby was that he was ticked at me and going to find me if it took him all day and here he was. Incredibly focused for a borderline psychopath.

"What do you want, Steve?"

Steve's bleary eyes flicked from me to

James. "It's my boy. Kent. You can't keep him away from me."

"As long as you continue to violate the terms of your parole, you have no right to see him."

Steve's eyes narrowed and he leaned closer. I wasn't going to take a step back and show weakness, but my insides were quaking. Steve was the kind of guy that could so easily jump either way.

"You tell your brother to stay away from my Juanita."

"What brother?" Steve's sudden change of topic confused me.

"That Chip dude. He's been seeing my girl, Juanita. The mother of my son." Steve sneered at me. "And you know I'm gonna see my kid. You shouldn't stop me if you know what's good for you." He pressed his finger against my chest and then I did take a step back, angry at how easily he could intimidate me.

Steve glanced from me to James, who stood quietly beside me. James easily had six inches and twenty pounds on Steve, but he said and did nothing. I felt a frisson of disappointment. Of course, who was I to complain. My brothers had raised me to take care of myself. Still, at the risk of sounding all damsel-like, I wouldn't have minded some intervention.

"I think you better leave," James said, finally stepping forward. Okay, not exactly Indiana Jones, but at least he made an attempt.

Steve's noxious grin showcased his crooked and missing teeth. He glanced at James again, seemingly satisfied that nothing was going to happen in that quarter.

"Yeah," he said. "I think I will." Then he turned and strode away, still weaving, but clearly feeling in charge of his world.

I drew in a long, slow breath, trying to assimilate what Steve had told me. Chip should have let me know he was seeing Juanita.

"That was close," James said, patting me on my shoulder. "Do you have to deal with guys like this all the time?"

"Once every two months." I felt another flicker of disappointment. I wished he would have let me lean against him—get some support for my wobbly legs.

"He's pretty intimidating." He put his hands on my shoulders. "You didn't seem the least bit scared of him."

"And the Oscar goes to…" I quipped. "I've learned that to show fear around these characters is to give them an edge. They're bullies, is all. I have to stand up to them. I'm glad you were here."

"I wish I could have done more, but I sensed that provoking him was not a good idea."

"You're right," I said. He had done exactly the right thing. Who knows what would have happened if Steve, slightly drunk and probably stoned, had decided to take up a challenge from James?

Yet why did I feel vaguely disappointed that James hadn't been more forceful?

James smiled down at me. "You're quite a woman, Danielle Hemstead," he said, sounding genuinely impressed.

"Just doing my job," I quipped, trying not to pay so much attention to how I could feel the warmth of his hands through my thin sweater and how I wished he would pull me close against his chest.

"I admire you for that." He squeezed my shoulders once again, then looked back over his shoulder. "Do you want to keep walking, or should I bring you back to your car? We don't want to run into that Steve guy again."

Steve was a bully. He had made his point so wouldn't be around for a while, but it would be a good idea not to take any chances. "Better walk me back to my car," I said with a look of regret.

As we strode back to our cars, we were both quiet. I wondered if James, who was enamored with Schubert's brusque and leisurely melodies, was put off by the seamier side of my job.

We got to my car without incident. I pulled my keys out of my purse, disappointed to see that my hands were shaking. "Are you sure you don't want a ride home?" he asked gently.

"No. I'll be fine."

Besides, my brothers were probably hanging around and I didn't want them to meet James. Yet.

"I had a wonderful time," he said after I got into the car. "I'd like to see you again."

Relief lifted my heart. I could do this again. "That would be nice."

"I'll call you tomorrow," he said. He bent over and for a moment I thought maybe he would kiss me. Instead he touched my hair with his hand, then straightened, and pushed the door closed.

As I drove away I could see him watching me. Then I turned a corner and he was gone.

He wants to see me again, I thought, as the memory of his good looks and his good smile sang through me on the drive home. I wished our evening could have been longer. I wished he could have driven me home.

It started raining by the time I pulled up behind Neil's truck. Thankfully, Chip and Jace were gone or I would have had to maneuver past their trucks, as well in my mad dash to the house. I stepped inside the house, shivering. The house was quiet. Dad was most likely in bed.

The papers that had been strewn all over the living room floor were gone and the furniture was all in its proper place.

Had someone come here to visit? Before I left, Neil and Jace had decided to oil their tack. Of course this had to be done in the living room so they could multitask—watch television and apply leather conditioner oil at the same time.

Out of curiosity, I checked the kitchen. The plates, though not in the dishwasher, were at least stacked on the counter.

I was immediately suspicious. The boys had never, ever, in all the years I have known them, bothered to so much as move plates from the table to the counter, let alone stack them up.

Those boys were up to something. Had to be. But what?

"My schedule has me busy up until late tonight—" James's deep voice was telling me over my office phone. I was on my lunch break so I had no guilt attached to his phone call. "—however, Saturday would work into my agenda."

I winced at his last word. There was *no* way I was going to let my brothers meet James until I knew exactly where I stood with him. My mind skipped back to Rodney, a previous boyfriend whom I had dated for a month before my brothers caught wind of the relationship and insisted that they meet him.

He had come for supper and afterward my brothers had taken him on a tour of the yard and gotten his new leather loafers dirty. When he'd come back, he was a changed man.

We'd gone out on one more date after that, but the poor guy was kind of jumpy. Then, he stopped calling. I found out from Chip afterward what had happened.

After the tour of the yard, my brothers had

sat him down on a straw bale in the old hip-roof barn and told him I had taken tae kwon do and knew how to handle a pistol. They made me sound like a cross between Thelma and Louise on their worst day.

So sweet my brothers were. So considerate. They told me they wanted to make sure Rodney knew I could take care of myself.

"Saturday works very well for me," I said, curling the phone cord around my finger, planning how I was going to keep my brothers out of the loop. I liked James, and I wasn't going to let my brothers mess this up.

I gave him my cell phone number and hung up, sighing with satisfaction. He seemed considerate. I loved his voice. And he was very, very easy on the eyes. Potential. Definite potential.

Before James called, I had been filling out my resume. Now, as I leaned my elbows on my hands I wondered if I was being too hasty.

It was too early to make a judgment on him, but I couldn't help wonder about his comment when he saw me praying. I so hoped he was a Christian so that I wouldn't have to make a hard decision there.

From the time my relationship with the Lord had become real and personal to me, I had made myself a promise that I would never date a man who didn't share my faith.

In a town like Preston, it wasn't too hard to separate the sheep from the wolves. If I had a file on them, stay away. Any others, I had either gone to school with or were related to.

When I went to college, I stuck with the pick-them-up-at-church-functions method, that, overall, had worked in terms of getting a date. In terms of getting a boyfriend, not so great. I was still single, wasn't I?

The phone rang and I was rescued from my analysis of my love life. The caller was Laurel Milligan, a single mother who I had been working with for a few weeks now. "Hey, Ms. Hemstead. Whaddya think? Should I be usin' cloth diapers on Hubie? My friend's stepmom told me they're better."

I couldn't help but laugh. Laurel thought I was an authority on the care and feeding of babies. I gave her what advice I could, which mainly consisted of referring her to the health nurse.

I hung up, added a few more sentences to the resume I had been working on. If I had a computer at home, I could do it there, but, alas, no such thing. I pulled a face at the vast white space on the screen. After college, this had been my one and only job, other than slinging hash in a diner in Edmonton to put myself through school—which was *not* going on the resume. The phone rang and I stifled a sigh. I was tempted to let the machine answer it, but that would mean I would end up having to listen to the message, write down the number and then return the call. Easier to simply answer it and get it over and done with.

"Child welfare. Danielle Hemstead speaking," I said absently, as I highlighted a section and hit the delete key.

"And? How was the date?" Tracy asked in her blunt manner. "Where did you go. What did you do?"

I smiled and leaned back in my chair, only too willing to indulge in the female pastime of rehashing a pleasant experience, analyzing it from all angles and getting a girlfriend's take on the night.

"We went to a movie, which wasn't great, but still fun. Then we went for a walk to the river." I avoided any reference to Steve. I needed to block that particular scene from my short-term memory. "James is a considerate man. And he likes poetry and listens to Schubert."

"Okay. And? Smooches?"

"No. Perfect gentleman."

"That doesn't sound too perfect to me. How could he resist your china blue eyes, your honey blond hair?"

I doodled a letter "J" on my memo pad. "He was being considerate."

"Is he a Christian?" Tracy's direct question made me laugh.

"He had said he admired me for praying before my meal in the restaurant. We didn't quite get to the salvation part of the evening."

"So when do I get to meet this guy or rather *man?*"

"Hey, give me a bit more time before I start bringing in the big guns."

"I'll be good. Guaranteed I'll be better than your brothers."

I wanted Tracy and David to meet him. I wanted to receive the blessing of my nearest and dearest friends. "Just let me get to know James a bit more. I might be disappointed."

"From the sound of your voice when you say his name, I think that might take a while."

"He is a nice man. In many ways."

"Well, keep me posted. Hey, the boss is here. I gotta run." I heard David's deep voice, then a light laugh as Tracy hung up.

I clicked the phone. A few days ago I would have suffered pangs of jealousy. But now...

Now I had the promise of another date and the hazy hope of a future relationship.

I spun around and faced my desk, and the picture of my brothers that I had clipped up on my in-box. It made me think of Chip.

I called the garage, but Neil told me he wasn't in and his cell phone said he was out of the service area. So I left a message that I would call him at 5:00 p.m.

I half-heartedly finished my resume as I ate my lunch, and before my coworkers started filing back into the office, my phone was ringing again and I was back to work. I didn't have a chance to think about James, our future date or my brothers or my application until Bobby looked in on me and told me she was leaving for the day.

I glanced at the clock on my computer. Five-thirty.

I tried calling Chip on his cell phone again, but it was off. My only other option was to stop by the arena. Neil had told me they were working some horses at the arena they used for their roping and riding practices and that they'd be late. He also told me not to bother stopping by.

This was a strange request. I never went to watch the boys do their guy, bonding thing anymore. I had spent enough of my youth hanging around ice rinks in the wintertime and roping and riding arenas in the summertime that I had reached maximum absorption.

I checked my messages again. There was one call from Jace to say that they'd be late for supper and, again, that I didn't need to come by the arena. I frowned.

My guy radar started spinning. My brothers had been acting weird the past few days. Their combined encouragement to stay away told me they were up to something and, perversely, that made me want to see *what* they were up to.

When I finished the last of the paperwork, I called home. Dad was fine. He was watching television. He didn't need me for a bit.

So at six-thirty, instead of going home, I headed for the arena where the boys were.

It had been drizzling when I left this morning, so driving down the road to the arena was almost a hazard. I fishtailed a couple of times, mud and dirt spraying up over my car.

When I got there, I parked by the row of trucks already lined up, mentally taking note of which ones were here. Chip's, Jace's and Neil's. All accounted for.

And a fourth one. A white truck. Just like the one that had been parked outside their shop when I stopped by there a few days ago. It had to belong to their buddy, Jigs.

Maybe that's why they wanted me to stay away. They knew I didn't like this guy very much.

Then I thought of the cleaned-up house last night. It had to be something else. My brothers were up to something and I needed to know what. *Now.*

So I got out of the car and hurried, as best as I could in my high heels, through the dirt to the arena.

As I came through the small side door I heard the clanging of a gate, the hollow sound of hooves hitting metal and the howling encouragement of the boys. Sounded like one of them was getting ready to work a bronc.

After my eyes adjusted to the gloom, I worked my way up to the observation area— a small rise of benches where girlfriends and family members watched their guys do what they loved. As a young girl I spent hours right here, waiting for my brothers while my mom drank coffee with other mothers and chatted and shared problems common to all farm wives.

I felt a nudge of nostalgia for those days, even though I usually grumbled and griped about having to come along. I wanted to stay home and play with my dolls or sew or embroider or read, but Mom didn't want me to be alone. So I came along and leaned on the rail, inhaled dust and dirt while my brothers pitted their brawn and brains against horses bred to buck.

"C'mon. He's a good un'," I heard Chip cry out. "Watch he don't spin on you." Jace added his advice, Neil his.

Their friend must be the one on the horse. Jigs.

I leaned over to see better, but all I saw of

the infamous Jigs was his hat, his dusty shirt straining over his broad shoulders and his gloved hands checking his rigging. It looked like he had already taken a few spills.

He gave a nod, Jace leaned over and swung open the gate and Jigs and the horse were out. The horse was a huge gelding named Truck Trouble. He was rough and big and loved to buck. And he was giving Jigs a good working over. Dust flew and I heard the grunt coming from the rider each time the horse landed. Truck Trouble spun and twisted, but Jigs kept his head low and stayed on, spurring him and getting a good rhythm.

Finally, Chip rang the bell, signaling eight seconds, and with a roar of pride Jigs leaped off the horse, landed on his feet and sent his hat into the air in the traditional gesture of victory.

"Way to go, Jigs," Jace called out.

As Jigs turned, he ran his gloved hands through his hair and looked up at me, his teeth a white slash of victory against his dusty skin.

And ice slipped through my veins.

Jigs was none other than my date of the other night. My Schubert-loving, poetry-spouting James Ashby.

Chapter Four

Dust floated down between us as James stared at me. All the vague hints and not-so-vague urgings to "stay away" and my brothers' parting comments about a bet that day at the garage came crashing together with a mind-numbing jar. Of course they wanted me to stay away. They didn't want me to discover their little plan to get Jigs—James, whoever—and their sister together.

On top of that, they probably wanted a detailed play-by-play of how dead easy it was to fool their romantic sister. I had heard enough recaps of dates over the breakfast table or dinner table to know exactly what their conversation had covered.

My imagination was making my cheeks

burn and my blood pressure rise. And James, whoever he was, was in on the whole thing.

How could I have been so incredibly dumb? And how could my brothers do this to me? Again.

Freddie Cramer, aka Fearless Freddie, in December, 1995, was the last time they had made a bet on me. I was heartbroken because I didn't have a date for the annual Preston Composite High School Frosty Formal. When Freddie asked me out I was ecstatic. Then I found out that my brothers had made a bet with Freddie and another friend. I could have walked away from that situation with my pride intact had I been the prize. Instead I found out that the loser had to take me.

I didn't talk to my brothers until the Christmas Eve service when the minister encouraged us to pass the peace. I would have preferred to pass a few other things, like a good smack, but the peace of Christmas had descended on me and I was in a mood to be generous.

I got a bit of my own back, though. The boys' punishment was being sent to the cosmetics counter of a local department store. Mom made them buy my favorite perfume, lotion and other assorted feminine products.

As far as I knew, they never did it again. Until now. And this time I didn't have Mom to help me out with the punishment.

Anger vied with shame and, much as it bothered me to admit it, a sharp dose of pain. I had *liked* this guy—man—well, actually, guy. While not exactly gearing up to register at Linens-n-Things, I was daring to doodle plans for future dates based on a pleasant evening.

What a fool I was.

So I crossed my arms, rooted to the spot by flimsy pride as James/Jigs vaulted over the side of the arena and ran up toward me. "Hey, Danielle," he called out, his voice full of pleasure. And why wouldn't it be? He had me fooled with his Schubert and his poetry and his nice suit. He had won.

At least Fearless Freddie had had the grace to look somewhat sheepish when I confronted him.

"So, how much did my brothers get you for?" I asked in my best imitation of my mom. I had to jump immediately on the defensive or my voice was going to start that little wobble thing that always drove my brothers nuts.

James pulled his hat off and frowned.

"What are you talking about?" His hair, now free from the constricting gel that had held his hair in place last night, fell across his forehead. It looked longer. Softer.

Are you a complete idiot? This character had some old-fashioned guy fun with your brothers at your expense and you're admiring the fact that today he's not using hair products?

I pushed the anger back into my voice. "The bet. Did they have to convince you to take it?"

"What are you talking about?"

He was *really* good. He had that whole innocent thing down pat. Some of my more delinquent foster kids could take lessons from him.

"C'mon, Jigs," I said, putting extra emphasis on the nickname my brothers used for him. "I know exactly what's been going on here."

Last night his smile had made me kind of trembly, made me feel all feminine and attractive.

Now, as he absently brushed sawdust off the crown of his hat, he gave me a slightly mocking grin, which made it easier to stoke the fires of my righteous indignation.

In spite of all those years of teasing and

tormenting, it still hurt that my brothers would resort to this again. And that they had managed to coach James so well that for a few hours I had actually thought I had met a potentially caring, sensitive man.

"Let me guess how this worked," I said, my anger building. "I didn't exactly fall all over you when they introduced us at the garage. Your pride was hurt so you and the boys got together and figured out the best way to get to me. Hence the haircut, the clean-shaven look, the suit…" I paused to let this all sink in to his "guy" brain. "Whose idea was the poetry? *That* was a nice touch."

James shrugged casually, not the slightest hint of shame in his expression. "Glad you liked it."

"It was inspired." I spat the words out, glared at my brothers, then back at James, or rather, Jigs. "And now I know why my brothers were so eager for me to stay away from here. How long were you hoping to keep this up before you sprung this on me. A week? A month? Did you have the meter ticking?" I stopped because I could feel the faint prick of tears in my eyes. I took a deep breath and got to my finale. "I hope you and my brothers got a good laugh out of the whole business. I hope you enjoyed yourself. And I hope I never see you again." I spun around and stormed back out of the arena, which was tricky considering I was wearing two-inch heels and the floor was dirt.

Of course there were no violins, wind machines or slow-motion camera shots. Of course James didn't call out my name and come running after me to tell me that I had it all wrong or that he was sorry.

This wasn't a romantic movie. This was a reality show—Danielle and Her Brothers. And the reality was that my coat caught on the door as I swung it open and a breeze coming in from outside tossed my long hair into my eyes and ended up reducing the impact of my supposedly dramatic exit.

What made it even worse, what really added to the perfection of the moment, was that as I was pushing my hair back so I could see to free my coat, I heard James—no, make that *Jigs*—call out, "Well, that went well."

I had coached Laurel Milligan through childbirth. I learned all about the breathing technique that was supposed to help her relax and I used it now.

I had to, or I would have left the coat hanging on the door while I went inside and performed violence on any male within hitting distance.

It was *not* my best moment.

"It's not fair, Lord," I wailed, as I drove home, thumping the steering wheel for emphasis, much like a preacher would the pulpit to drive a point home. "I finally think I find a decent man and he ends up in cahoots with my brothers. And I know I'm not supposed to hate him or them, but right now my grapes of wrath are being trampled. Hard. Why are they always so miserable to me? Why can't they treat me like a sister instead of like a buddy?" Then, in spite of my pique, I added, "And why couldn't that James person have turned out to be a nice man who would care for me and be all sensitive and give me flowers and buy pretty presents for my birthday instead of windshield wiper fluid for my car, like the boys do?"

I sniffed, which made me feel like a quavery teenager and only added to my frustration. I was a grown woman. I had been hardened in the crucible of living with my brothers. Being a sob-sister was not tolerated.

"Sorry, Lord," I added as I pulled into the

driveway of our home. "I don't mean to be complaining and I know I don't have anything to kvetch about, but it sure would be nice to be treated a little better by the males in my life." I waited a moment, letting my emotions settle down. Then, when I was over my mini-pique, I added a prayer for my father and for some of the harder cases I'd had to deal with in the past week.

I thought again of Kent, who, thanks to Tracy's intervention, was now in a safe foster home while his mother got her life back on track. Apparently with Chip.

And I was so busy defending my honor that I forgot to talk to Chip about Juanita. And Steve. I had to remember to tell him, or I was going to end up caught in the crossfire.

As I entered the house, I heard the excited voice of a sports commentator describing an amazing catch some outfielder had made while playing some game somewhere.

I paused in the door of the living room, but Dad didn't look up. Of late, my father didn't take kindly to distractions and I doubted I would get a sympathetic ear if I told him what his sons had done to me. So I slouched off to my bedroom to pout in private.

As I changed I caught my reflection in the mirror. I brushed my long, blond hair back from my face and took a moment to study my face. Sort of pretty, if you liked the pale look. Ordinary nose, mouth needed lipstick. Eyes, okay, as long as I put mascara on the pale eyelashes.

Had James seen anything he liked about me?

I thought again of his comment when I came into the garage, his look at the supermarket checkout. How he smiled at me when we were at the restaurant. How he looked at me when we walked toward the river.

The almost kiss I got.

I spun away from the mirror. What did I care what some guy-friend of my brother's thought about me. I was a joke, a bet, a deal, a challenge. Pick one.

I walked into the living room and laid my hand on my dad's shoulder. He looked up at me. "You're home late. Busy day at work?"

"How are you feeling?"

He lifted his hand and waggled it back and forth. "Tired, but not too bad." He patted my hand, then turned his attention back to the baseball game. I stood a moment, watching as the batter walked up to the plate, tapped it, spat and hitched his pants up, while the commentator delivered an incomprehensible barrage of information about him. I liked to participate in the dinner conversation, so occasionally I made an effort to watch.

I shifted my weight, glancing back over my shoulder at the clock. Enough with the sports bonding moment. I had to get supper going.

"I'll be in the kitchen if you need me," I said to my father.

As I peeled potatoes, scraped carrots and fried chicken, my mind kept slipping back to the humiliation of the afternoon. Was I so desperate that I jumped on any available male without being even slightly suspicious?

And what was to be suspicious of? I thought James was on the level. I thought he was a nice person. A stranger in town who respected my faith, who could talk for five minutes without mentioning anything remotely resembling a sports statistic.

I cringed all over again when I remembered the conversations I'd had with him. Especially my "man" and "guy" rant. He must have had a great laugh with my brothers over that one.

And my brothers? Didn't they care about

me at all? Were my feelings simply something to have fun with?

As my thoughts spun around and around, my blood started to boil. I looked at the potatoes, now covered with water, waiting until the boys were home before I cooked them.

I made a radical decision.

No more waiting, like Mom always did, for them to come home before I started cooking the vegetables. No more waiting until they were done washing their hands before I put the dressing on the Caesar salad so the croutons wouldn't get soggy.

Until I officially moved out, supper was going to be served on my schedule, not the other way around. I put the carrots on the stove and turned on the heat under them with a vicious twist of my wrist.

You rebel, you.

I set the table and then joined my father.

"How soon is supper, honey?"

"In about twenty minutes."

"Are the boys here yet?"

"Doesn't matter. Dinner's ready in twenty, we're eating in twenty."

This netted me a puzzled glance but I didn't respond. I had made up my mind and

I wasn't going to yield. Fifteen minutes later I got up to do the last-minute preparations when I heard the back door slam, and my brothers' voices, and disappointment pressed on my tired brain.

What was the use of trying to make a point when the people didn't stay away long enough for the point to be made?

Jace, Chip and Neil burst into the kitchen, laughing and joking. I stood with my back to them, ignoring them, but they didn't break ranks or pace, and headed straight for the bathroom to wash up. No remorse. No, "Gee, sister, I'm sorry we messed with your mind and your heart."

Just a faint reduction of chatter as they passed by me.

I poured the water off the carrots and put the pot on the table. Life. It was the same old, same old. I really *had* to get out of here.

"Chip, you need to know Juanita is not someone you can fool around with. She's in a fragile place. I don't want you going out with her and then changing your mind. Besides, this Steve guy is not someone you want to fool around with. You be careful." I adjusted the hands-free headset of my phone as I put the finishing touches on my resume. It was Wednesday, after hours, so I didn't have to feel guilty about using government time. The job I was applying for looked like a dream job—working for an international adoption agency. Some travel was required. Boy, howdy, did that sound like the job for me. Travel was exactly the thing I needed right now. I was ready to geographically extend the boundaries of my life.

My big talk with my brothers Friday night had fizzled into a complaint about their matchmaking, which wasn't really the issue. They couldn't understand my pique. So instead of three groveling contrite brothers I got The Look and The Shrug.

My anger with them made me forget to talk to Chip about Juanita. Until now.

"Steve is mean, he's trouble and he's out to get you."

"I'm not afraid of him," Chip said. "I'll take my chances. As for Juanita, I like her. I met her a while ago and I know she's had her share of problems, but I really care about her and that little boy."

"Do you really know what you're getting

into?" I was pleased that my brother didn't see Kent as a liability. I really liked the kid myself and wanted badly for him to have some stability in his life.

"I think I do. Juanita does, too. She's tough and she's trying to get her life together."

Tough. The ultimate compliment from my brothers.

"Even Jigs was afraid of Steve," I added, my voice heavy with innuendo.

"Juanita told me enough about Steve," Chip said. "She said he was a bully. I'd like to see her move out of town, away from him. By the way, did we ever get a renter for the old house?"

I secretly hoped we wouldn't get a response to any ad. My practical and thrifty brothers wanted to tie into the existing power and gas lines and had built our new house a stone's throw from the old one. Depending on who threw the stones. At any toss, I liked the privacy of not having any one else on the yard.

"No. I thought Neil was going to put an ad in the paper."

"I don't know if he did, but if the house is empty… Hey, I gotta go."

The dial tone in my ear signaled the end of

another scintillating conversation with my younger brother. Was he looking for a place for Juanita? I hoped not. I was on the hit list of enough other parents of kids in care that the last thing I needed was to have a viable target living right on the yard. I wasn't her caseworker so I didn't know what her situation was. But if she needed a place to stay, it wouldn't be very Christian of me to turn her down.

I was about to pull the headset off when the phone rang again. I glanced at the clock. The office was officially closed, but an innate sense of responsibility had me answering before my tired mind could process the word "no."

"Hello, Danielle? How are you?"

The deep voice sent my heart into a long, slow flip. Then my brain fired up again. "Oh, just fine, Jigsy," I said through tight lips. "Been listening to some Schubert lately."

"Schubert is good. Highly underrated."

"Nice. What can I do for you?" Jigs/James had left a number of messages the past few days, none of which I was inclined to respond to. But he had caught me now and I was forced to be reasonably civil.

"I thought I'd call. See how you were doing."

"Let's see. Heart is good. Blood pressure

a bit up, but that's understandable given my job. Iron count is low, but as for the rest, I'm fine. And my goodness, look at the time, I have to run." Then I hung up.

I yanked the earphones off my head, wishing my little rebellion made me feel more empowered than it did. When I finally got myself back on track I continued working on my resume, wishing I could add more experience than this single job. Then, with a nothing-ventured, nothing-gained exhortation ringing through my head, I put it all together in a neat little package.

My hand hesitated on the Send button. Did I dare leave my father in the care of my brothers? Did I dare stay around and slowly wither away?

I bit my lip, said a quick prayer, then hit the Enter key and sent it off into cyberspace. Now my resume and application were someone else's responsibility. As for Dad, I just had to pray that if the Lord wanted me to have this job, He'd help me find a way to take care of Dad.

"Great supper, Dani." Jace wiped his mouth, pushed his plate away and glanced at Neil with raised eyebrows.

Neil looked up from scraping up the last of the ice cream from his bowl. "Yeah. Really good. Thanks."

"Is this a new kind of ice cream?" Chip asked. "It's really good."

"Yes, like the pizza you finished, I bought it all by myself," I said, secretly pleased that they were at least trying to make amends for their bad behavior the other day.

"So, Dad, Chip said he talked to you about the old farmhouse on the yard here," Jace said, glancing from Neil to Chip to our dad.

"You want to rent it out," he said, finishing off the last of his soup. I didn't dare feed him the artery-clogging pizza, so had made him his favorite tomato soup. Thankfully he wasn't fussy. "Fine by me."

"How about you, Danielle?" Chip glanced at me. "How do you feel? It would be a good thing to do. Be neighborly."

I was surprised they asked me, but I saw it as a positive move in a good direction. It would give me a chance to help Juanita out and help keep an eye on her. "I wasn't really keen on it at first, but if everyone else agrees, I'm okay with it. After all, my job is all about helping people and giving them a chance to turn their life around. If that's going to happen, then I'm okay with it."

"Okay," Jace said, drawing out the word as he lifted one puzzled eyebrow. "Just making sure."

"Great." Chip sat back, relief in his voice. "I'm glad you changed your mind about Jigs."

I frowned. "Jigs? How did the conversation go from renting the house to Juanita to Jigs."

Chip's smile faded to a puzzled look. "Juanita's not renting the house. Jigs is."

Chapter Five

"You guys are seriously deranged," I said, glaring at each one of them to make my point.

Chip frowned, uncomprehending. Neil grinned and shrugged. Only Jace had the sense to look a shade embarrassed.

"I don't want him staying here," I said in my best "don't mess with me" voice.

"Dani, the roof on the house he's living in is leaking," Chip put in, giving me his best puppy-dog look, ignoring my pithy outburst.

I looked from Neil to Chip to Jace but they were all smiling at me. What was it about Jigs that had my brothers so staunchly on his side? I had never seen them take someone so firmly under their wing before.

I finally turned to my father to appeal to

him. "Dad, I don't think it is such a good idea to have a strange man on our yard."

"He's not strange." Dad frowned at me. "I thought you went on a date with him."

Which was why I didn't think it was such a good idea to have strange man on our yard.

"How long does he need a place?" I grudgingly asked, realizing I was cornered.

"Just until he gets his roof fixed," Neil said, grinning at me.

"Which you guys are going to do, right?"

"Of course."

I looked from brother to brother and had an ominous feeling. This was not going to go well.

I wasn't going to watch, I thought, yanking another weed out of the flower bed. I was going to stay focused on the job at hand and not let my emotions get the better of me.

I tossed a large stinkweed over my shoulder. Then another. Last fall I had been too busy to clean up the flower beds. This meant I now had to hunt through a jungle of weeds to find the perennials. My mother had planted most of them and at one time her flower beds had been her pride and joy.

Now they were humblingly depressing. A

testament to my life spent in an office hunting down delinquent parents and deadbeat dads on the phone instead of out in the hale and hearty outdoors.

I needed to get at these flower beds before I forgot what was in them and my brothers took a propane torch to the entire works. They believed in a scorched-earth policy when it came to weeds and hadn't grasped the whole selective weeding concept.

Even though I was engrossed in my project I easily heard the sounds coming from the little house below us.

"Hey, careful with the couch." I heard a too familiar voice call out. "It's vintage."

"Isn't that just a fancy word for junk?" Neil called back.

"It's only junk if it's in the landfill," James said.

"Isn't that a fancy name for dump?"

This had been going on ever since the white-and-orange rental truck had pulled up to the other house at 6:00 a.m. this morning. I had tried to sleep through the noise of talking and laughter, but my window overlooked the yard and the sound carried up the hill. At 7:00 a.m. I had finally given up and gotten out of bed.

Today was the first Saturday in weeks that I wasn't on call, and I had been looking forward all week to sleeping in, then leisurely working on the yard, possibly taking my horse, Spook, out for a ride. I had been neglecting him of late and the guilt I felt about that was one more notch on my belt. And, up until a week ago, I had been looking forward to spending some time with James. Snake.

I yanked another weed out and tossed it over my shoulder. And another and another, and then had to stop myself because the last "weed" I had pitched was a shoot from one of Mom's favorite lilies.

About fifteen minutes later I had all four flower beds in front of the house done and, in spite of my frustration, was quite pleased with the result. I could easily make out the new spikes of green from the rest of the lilies, the mound of leaves of the columbine and the shoots of the iris and poppies. The other perennials would show themselves later.

"Do you have a broom?"

I screamed, jumped, then spun around.

James's hair was spiked with sweat, whiskers stubbled his chin, dirt smudged his face and a pink T-shirt strained across his broad chest and shoulders. His blue jeans were ripped at one knee and he wore sneakers with the laces trailing.

It was a combination of anger and surprise that made my heart quiver, I assured myself as I planted my fists on my hips.

"A broom?" Oh, you witty and intelligent creature, you. Did you think of that all by yourself?

"Yeah. You know." He pretended to make a sweeping motion. "Gets rid of dirt with a flick of the wrist?" Then he smiled. Just like he did when I first met him. Just like he did on our date.

"I forgot mine," he continued, his smile slipping in the face of my obvious displeasure. Just like it did when I discovered his true identity as a snake. "Well, actually, I don't have one. There's no substitute for a true lack of preparation so I'm counting on you to help me out."

He was making me feel edgy and nervous. "Sure. I have a broom. Somewhere." I turned, took a step and promptly got tangled up in the pile of weeds I had accumulated.

Strong hands caught me by my arm.

In a really good romantic movie he would

have caught me by both arms, I would have ended up standing face-to-face with him, so close we could have kissed....

Instead I was thrown off balance and I ended up with his hand clamped around my upper arm and me on one knee on the weeds. Very delicate. Very romantic.

Very infuriating.

I jerked my arm away, but James held on, pulling me to my feet.

"Sorry about that," he said, with an apologetic look.

I brushed my arm, brushing away the feel of his hand on mine, but it didn't disappear as quickly as I would have liked. "I'll get your broom."

I found one on the back porch and brought it out to him. He was standing in front of the flower beds, looking down at the plants.

"So what are these?" he asked, pointing to the lilies.

"Asiatic lilies." I shoved the broom toward him. I wasn't about to give him another chance to spout off information that would make him look all sensitive and caring. "Do you need anything else?"

I knew I was being rude and abrupt, but

he made me feel unsettled. Too many confusing emotions were attached to this guy—attraction and frustration and anger and glimmers of hope.

I waited a beat, then walked back toward the house.

Please, Lord, help me to be civil to him, I prayed as I jerked open the door of the porch. *And please, Lord, help me not to fall for him again.* Literally and figuratively.

Over the course of the morning, Chip, Jace and Neil were in and out of the house borrowing window cleaner, a mop, the vacuum cleaner, garbage bags, boxes and, for some inexplicable reason, the cordless phone.

I got the weeds dragged away and then started up the riding lawn mower in a futile attempt to drown out the noise I heard coming from the house. Someone had turned a stereo on and they were playing Keith Urban at full decibel.

Nice try, I thought as I spun around the yard, not falling for the obvious ploy.

An hour later the lawn was mowed, I had trimmed the edges along the flower beds and the sidewalk and I was hot and sweaty. The stereo next door was still going strong.

Over the noise I heard sounds of hammering and the whine of a jigsaw. Were they renovating?

As I hung up the Weed Eater in the garage, I forced down my innate curiosity. I didn't need to know what they were up to, but I did need my broom to sweep away the grass. So how could I get it without physically going down there?

Brainwave. I could get Dad to get it and use the excuse that I was making lunch for him.

Brushing the grass clippings off my pants, I toed off my runners and went looking for my dad to get me off the hook.

I found him in his recliner. Asleep. For a moment I tried to reconcile the tired, old man laying in his chair with the vital and alive father who used to go riding with me or take me out on long hikes. The man who would wrestle large, unruly calves when we had to give them shots before putting them out on pasture.

The doctors had warned me, but I couldn't have imagined the change that had come over my father since his heart attack.

I pulled the newspaper off his chest, folded it and put it on the coffee table. As I stroked the hair away from his face I thought of the resume and application I had sent off a couple of days ago.

If I got the job did I dare leave him in my brothers' hands?

If I didn't, did I dare stay around?

The phone rang and I jumped to answer it before its shrill tones woke up my father. I checked the call display as I connected and my heart dropped to my shoes. It was my boss.

"Hey, Casey. What can I do for you?"

"I just got wind of an emergency apprehension and placement." Was it me, or did he sound even happier than he should have?

"But it's my first Saturday off in weeks," I whined. "Get Henry Agnew to do it. He's on call." And, I wanted to add, more capable of dealing with all the potential for disaster that came with apprehensions.

"I can't get hold of him and this is an emergency. A baby and a two-year-old. We have to move while we can."

What was this, irresponsible parent week?

If it wasn't for the fact that I wanted—no, *needed*—this other job and, by extension, a good reference from Casey, I would have told him no. Told him to try harder at tracking down Henry and send him to do some real work. But Casey knew I wanted to move on and he was using my situation to his advantage.

Instead I stifled my frustration and anger. "Where's this supposed to happen?" I asked, pulling out a pen and paper to take directions.

"Sangudo."

A two-hour drive away. I wouldn't be home till midnight, which meant poor Spook would have to wait for yet another free day to get some exercise. As I jotted down the relevant information I glanced at my father. My previous reluctance to leave him for another job was now balanced with the stark reality of my current job and my current boss. I couldn't get away from either fast enough.

There wasn't much in the refrigerator for supper. No handy leftovers that I could get the boys to heat up for Dad and themselves. No pizza in the freezer. I fell back on an old staple. Bean soup in the slow cooker. I quickly dumped the ingredients in the pot, one eye on the clock, then ran upstairs to change.

I slipped on slacks, a soft shirt and a blazer. Low shoes. I never knew what to expect with these apprehensions. I knew that I usually needed to combine the ability to leap over couches in a single bound with a semiprofessional look.

I brushed my hair, pulled it back, put on some makeup and gave myself a critical look. Okay. Time to head into battle. But first, I had to go down to the house and let my brothers know what was going on, which meant facing James again.

The music had been turned down by the time I got there. The hammering had stopped, but the boys were still laughing together. I knocked on the door and Jace yelled at me to come on in.

Chip, Jace, Neil and James were seated around the kitchen table going through what looked like James's photo albums.

"Hey, come on in," James said, looking up at me with a smile.

"What's up, sis?" Neil asked. His long blond hair was anchored with a baseball cap that was sprinkled with wood shavings.

"I have to go to work." I wasn't going to look. I wasn't curious about James's house. But in spite of my determination to keep myself aloof, I couldn't help a glance around. The living room looked surprisingly cozy. A couch and two matching chairs. I saw what the boys had been working on. Between the two large living room windows sat a bookshelf, its wood still gleaming white. It was already filled with books.

The variety of appliances on the kitchen counter surprised me. I think the only kitchen appliance my brothers could correctly identify was the toaster.

"Casey called," I continued. "I need to do an emergency apprehension and placement. I want one of you to go up to the house once in a while and see how Dad is doing. Maybe keep him company." I fidgeted with the strap of my briefcase, trying to avoid James's looking at me, but in spite of that, I was more aware of his presence than I was of my brothers. "I made some bean soup. It's in the slow cooker."

"Can James have some?" Neil asked.

"Sure. Whatever."

"I thought this was your weekend off?" James asked.

"I did, too," I said, checking my cell phone to make sure I had enough juice in the battery. "But apparently Casey seems to think I'm the only one that can do this particular job." I zipped my briefcase shut and finally looked up at him. He was sitting sideways, his elbow resting on the table, his hazel eyes holding mine.

"You should have told him you were busy."

I held his gaze a moment, surprised that he cared. "Maybe I should have." The only problem was, I hadn't been working long enough to accumulate enough years of experience to speak to any future employer. I was counting on my willingness to work when I could to balance that deficiency.

"Be careful you don't burn yourself out."

His words, spoken in a quiet voice and combined with the intent look in his eyes, softened my resistance to him and kindled a soft glow of pleasure. His concern was an unfamiliar experience for me.

Then I saw Jace nudge James's foot under the table and caught Neil giving James an elbow. Chip winked at him.

For sincerity, judge number one, 5.6.

"Thanks for the tip," I said icily. "I'll keep it in mind."

There it was again. A flicker of puzzlement that was either staged or real. I didn't want to spend too much time trying to decipher it.

James was officially filed away as a mistake that I wasn't about to repeat.

I left. But as I drove, I found myself remembering his concern, staged or otherwise, wishing it didn't resurrect old yearnings and desires.

I knew I was a romantic, something that living with three brothers, a gruff father and a no-nonsense mother hadn't been able to root out of my life. I loved melancholy music, sad stories, fairy tales, ruffles, lace and delicate things. Sometimes I was convinced I wasn't really a Hemstead. That I had been switched in the hospital and somewhere there was an elegant woman who was dealing with a rough, tough tomboy daughter who hated dolls when she was young, chewed gum and wore leather and denim.

And my romantic nature, in spite of my rough and tumble upbringing, yearned for someone who would cherish and pamper me. Who would care that a foster kid had punched me in the face. Who would make appropriately sympathetic noises and give me a hug and stroke my hair when I'd had an especially emotional day.

My brothers didn't always have time to hear

my stories or the emotional space to really care. My father used to listen but I could always tell that his mind was elsewhere.

Even Tracy didn't always understand.

Tracy had lived an independent life. Her mother had been an absent parent and Tracy had practically raised herself. When she moved to Preston, we became friends, and after that she was at our house whenever her mother wasn't around, which was fairly often. But Tracy was tough and it had taken David's kindness to wear away that veneer and win her heart.

I grew up with guys who laughed at my tears and still didn't "get" my emotions. Hence my desire for a man. Hardly the goal that suffragettes and the women's movement had made sacrifices for. But I had learned that no matter how tough the woman, no matter how difficult the life, many of them wanted the same thing I did.

Someone who was willing to put her first. Someone who really needed her.

As I drove, I prayed for my father. Prayed that he would regain his health and that he would regain his zest for life. Prayed that he would get healthy enough that I could leave him in the hands of my brothers and not feel guilty.

Casey's directions were erratic, to say the least. It took me seven stops to redefine the parameters of my search and by the time I got there, the sun was drifting toward the horizon. The family was living in a mobile home parked at the end of a graveled road and I was thankful for the lack of neighbors. Usually I got all kinds of good and bad advice on what I could do with myself and my department and my decision to interfere with these poor people's lives.

So helpful.

I knocked on the door and got no answer. The door was open, and all I heard coming from inside was the heart-rending wails of a crying baby and another kid humming over the ubiquitous noise from the television.

The smell inside was sadly familiar. Alcohol, stale carpet and the funky scent of air that had been trapped in one place too long.

The mother of the two children lay sleeping or passed out on the couch. The baby girl was crying in a crib in one corner of the living room. Closer inspection showed me that she was soaked from head to toe and the little boy sat naked on the living room floor eating a cold hot dog. No father or male "partner" was anywhere in sight. Big surprise.

Just another day in paradise.

Thankfully I had an emergency kit with me—disposable diapers, extra clothes and Gummi Bears—and dealt with the kids while Momma snored on. I woke her up and explained what I was doing, who I was.

As I was showing her the paperwork, I saw a shadow out of the corner of my eye. A huge shadow filling the doorway.

Grandpa, I thought with dismay as I looked up.

But it was a large woman, wearing a dress that had the ever popular breaking-up-the-food-fight pattern seen on the runways in Milan this year. What really caught my attention was what she had accessorized her outfit with. A large, wooden baseball bat.

It wasn't fair, I thought, glancing at my soft leather briefcase. All it held was a cell phone, a PDA, some leftover candies, papers and my car keys. Hardly an even match.

"Who are you? Whatcha doin'?" Her voice was surprisingly pleasant. Of course, she could afford to be affable. She had the upper hand, or rather, upper baseball bat.

I put on my sternest voice, hoping to intimidate with attitude where I couldn't with weaponry. "I'm a social worker. My name is Danielle Hemstead and I've been given the authority to remove these children from this woman's care."

She narrowed her eyes, but thankfully lowered the baseball bat. "You're not the same worker we've been seeing around here."

"No. That worker couldn't come." That worker was probably enjoying the usual Saturday night fun—laughing, socializing— all the while his cell phone conveniently turned off.

I needed to get myself more of a life so I could be busy when Casey was trolling the phone lines looking for likely suspects.

I pulled out my paperwork and showed it to her, then flashed her my ID and gave her my card. "You are welcome to call the RCMP and double check." We always called the local detachment in advance in case we needed backup. Or in situations like this. I was keeping my eye on the baseball bat while she looked over my papers.

"Okay," she said, handing the whole business back to me. "I'm glad you people are finally doing something. It took you long enough."

Of course it did, I thought as I folded up a copy of the notice and slipped it in an envelope. If we waited too long to apprehend, we were negligent. If we came too soon we weren't giving the mother a chance. If something really serious happened, it was our fault.

Never mind that Mommy dearest was laying on the couch in a stupor while her kids cried and scrounged for food. She was simply a victim. And Daddy? Well, he was where most of these guys are. Gone.

The baby cried the entire two-hour trip back to Preston. The little boy sat in the booster seat I carried with me in case of emergencies and stared out the window. Sorry as I felt for the little guy, I couldn't leave him where he was. If he were older I might have tried to explain that to him. As it was all I could do was feed him a few Gummi Bears and try to tell him where we were going and what I was doing. If it registered, I don't know.

By the time I dropped the kids off at the receiving home, I had a splitting headache and I was feeling the weight of the world's sorrow. Sometimes I wondered if I felt too deeply. Other times I wondered if I was getting too hardened. Today felt like a combination of both.

I chose to focus on the wonderful family of father, mother and older children who had come running out when I came—arms reaching for the little lost souls I had brought them. They were God's hands and feet on earth, I thought as I handed over the screaming baby and the puzzled toddler. When I drove away, I knew, for now, those little children would be loved and cared for. But I also knew that the mother of the children would be given a chance to get her life back together. If things went really well, the mother would take what was given her and make a change. If they didn't, I'd be seeing those kids again in a year. Maybe less.

Which made me think of Juanita. Kent's foster parents had been a guiding force in her life. They had given Kent a safe place while Juanita learned to make better decisions.

And now my brother was dating her. I really wanted to sit down with him and make it crystal clear what the implications of dating this fragile woman could be. Not to mention the real possibility that Steve, Kent's biological father, could come after him with a gun.

Oh, the glamorous life of a child welfare worker, I thought as I pulled into the driveway. As I passed the old house, I noticed that a light was on in James's room.

Probably reading poetry, I thought, parking my little car beside Chip's monstrously large tow truck. Or listening to Schubert.

I turned off the engine and blasted out a few sighs, releasing all the stale air, letting myself wind down. I was bone weary and wanted to have a shower, but didn't think I would have the energy.

I opened the door and slowly got out of the car, taking a moment to stretch out my stiff muscles.

A voice broke out of the darkness. "Bad day?"

I screamed.

Chapter Six

My heart leapt into my throat as I whirled to face this new menace, wondering what I could use as a weapon.

James stood by the back fender of my car, his hands up in a gesture of surrender, his features cast into shadows by the watery light of the moon. In spite of that, I still saw the glint of his eyes and the faint smile of his mouth. "I'm sorry. I thought you saw me coming."

Stop heart. Slow down. But it wouldn't obey. Of course it didn't help that in spite of the nasty trick he and my brothers had played on me I still found him moderately attractive. Okay, very attractive.

I was not a credit to my species. "I was in

my car," I retorted, taking refuge in some semblance of anger. "How could I have seen you?"

"Rearview mirror?" he suggested, lowering his hands.

"You give me too much credit for being observant." I dragged in a long breath, as my heart downshifted. One heart patient in the family was one too many. "Why are you sneaking around?"

"I heard your car drive up. I wanted to see if you were okay."

"You were checking up on me?"

He nodded, slipped his hands in his back pockets and rocked back on his heels. "Did everything go okay?" he continued, his deep voice going soft. "I mean with the kids and all?"

I thought of the concern he showed before I left. Was he really good at this kind of thing or was he for real?

"It wasn't my best moment. I don't enjoy taking kids away from their parents." I thought of my run-in with the fashion maven, but that was par for the course. At least she wasn't a relative threatening to sue.

"I imagine it can be difficult." He shifted his weight, moving closer to me. He raised his hand, then lowered it as if he had planned on touching me but changed his mind. "You look like you've been crying."

His concern sent me into a tailspin. Any of the men I had dated didn't want to talk about my job. My brothers assumed anyone who could stop pucks (I always played goal when they played pick up games of hockey) ride bareback (never enough saddles to go around) and jump-start a car (cheaper than fixing a wonky starter) could hold her own against drunk and/or cranky parents. So they never asked. "It's a regular thing in this job," I said casually, trying to shrug off his concern.

"But still, it's gotta be hard."

I was too tired to puzzle out intentions and read between potential pickup lines. So I chose the direct route. "It is hard. The kids, in spite of how lousy they are being taken care of and how poor the conditions, never want to leave their parents. In spite of how horrible the situation, it's the only life they've known. And what bothers me even more is their mother was probably raised the same way. Her kids are probably going back to her as soon as she finds a good legal aid lawyer and a counselor and tells them both that she's turning her life around. Again. So the kids will go back and we know that unless she has a good support system in place, she's going to fall back into the same bad behavior and on a good day the kids will be eating cold wieners and on a bad day, rooting through the garbage."

I was tired, stressed about my day, my dad, about my life. That was the only explanation I had for the way everything spilled out in my wobbly voice and how I was now seeing James through a shimmery curtain of unshed tears. I had done this countless times and though it made me sad, it didn't often make me cry.

I looked down and blinked, embarrassed to feel the warm slide of tears down my cheeks. "Sorry," I mumbled, trying to figure out how to wipe them away without looking like I was wiping them away. Guys hated the tears. "I've been too busy lately. Working too much."

Then James was beside me, his hand on my shoulder, his fingers gently kneading my skin. "It's okay. It's a hard job. But it's important and significant. I really admire what you do."

A pep talk now complete with a brotherly slap on the back?

But even as I tried to flippantly dismiss his touch, I was too aware of the warmth of his hand that felt anything but brotherly, and the faint scent of fresh cut wood that lingered on his clothes. For a split second I wanted to move a little closer. To lean against him and let his arms surround me and be strong for me.

You are such a sucker, mocked the voice of my cynical alter ego. *He tried the same thing on you a few days ago and you fell for it like a blind roofer.*

I pulled away. I palmed my tears off my cheek and gave him a curt nod. "I better go."

I turned and trudged up the stairs to the house. He was still standing by my car when I shut the porch light off and in the half light of the moon I saw him walk back to his little house.

As I got ready for bed I still couldn't figure out what to make of his nocturnal visit and hoped I wouldn't have to put up with many more. I didn't need him wandering in and out of my everyday life.

I switched on my beside lamp, slipped into bed and I was about to turn off my light when I caught sight of my Bible. I hadn't been reading as regularly as I should have. I had worked my way through the Old Testament and had finished Song of Solomon, which had only spurred on my romantic dreams. To imagine someone loving me as the writer had loved his "beloved." I knew God did and that the book was an allegory of God's love for us, but I still yearned for a love like that between me and a man. Did I mention that I was a romantic?

Now I was starting Isaiah, but I didn't know if I was in the mood for Old Testament justice, so I flipped to the New Testament. I found the marked passage of 1 Thessalonians 5:14 and started reading. *"And we urge you, brothers, warn those who are idle, encourage the timid, help the weak, be patient with everyone."* I stopped there a moment, thinking of the work I had done today. Like James had said, what I did was important work. But as for being patient with everyone, that was harder. Did Dad and my brothers fall into the "everyone" category?

My mother always said she understood my brothers more than me. Mom was the type of wife who pitched in and helped around the farm, assuming that most women felt the same, though she always said she felt more comfortable around men than women. When the boys drew mustaches and beards on my posters of Brad Pitt and Johnny Depp, my mother smiled and assured me they were just having fun. When they laughed at me for crying each time we watched my dad's favorite movies, *Old Yeller* or *Where the Red Fern Grows*, she would ruffle my hair and tell me they were just being boys.

Somehow, I was never just being a girl.

I read on.

"…encourage the timid, help the weak be patient with everyone. Make sure that nobody pays back wrong for wrong, but always try to be kind to each other and to everyone else. Be joyful always, pray continually, give thanks in all circumstances, for this is God's will for you in Christ Jesus."

Give thanks in all circumstances. Not so easy when circumstances seemed to be arrayed against me. I wanted my brothers to be more mature now so that I could leave Dad in their care and not worry that he would end up living off chips and pop and never leaving his recliner.

I hardly dared project too far into the future because if I did, all I saw was my ghostly figure in an old worn housedress, wearing a hair net and sagging support hose, dusting around three brothers who were watching television and burping.

I really needed to get out of here. But for now, I had prayed about it and I had let it go. It was in God's hands now.

I closed the worn Bible, turned off the light and stared out the window. Moonlight bathed my room in a light glow casting faint shadows. As I stared out the night, I heard the muffled noise of a truck door slamming. It came from the other house. James must still be loitering about.

Did I have a right to be angry with him?

He had raised hopes in me and dashed them and did it for some silly bet with my brothers. I knew I had to forgive him for my sake as much as his, but at the same time I would be foolish to trust him again.

"Could you come in for an interview next week?" the very nice man on the other end of my cell phone was asking me.

I was filling my cart in the grocery store with provisions for my supper company and had selected a luscious looking head of broccoli when the call came.

It wasn't my brothers, and it wasn't Casey,

all of whom I would have ignored in favor of the delicate job of choosing the perfect vegetable, so I answered it taking a chance that it would be some deranged client demanding that I come over. Now.

But to my surprise, delight and fear, it was the "Attention-Of" man I had sent my resume to. Dan Crittenden.

"Sure. That would be fine," I said in a bright voice, trying to absorb the reality of what one little click of a mouse button could set in motion.

"That's good. I look forward to seeing you then." He told me he would be e-mailing the address and time.

When the nice man hung up, I snapped my phone shut, feeling quavery and brave and concerned all rolled into one.

I had to trust that God would bring me where He wanted me, but I had to confess I was a little nervous at how quickly things were happening. I hadn't expected to hear from this place for another week.

Nor did I expect my phone to ring again before I could properly map out any possible scenario for my future. Neil, this time.

"Hey, what can I do for you?" I asked as I

pushed my buggy a little farther down the produce aisle, stopping at an artistically arranged assortment of peppers. I wanted to buy one of each, because they would look so pretty in my vegetable drawer.

"Are David and Tracy still coming for supper tonight?" he asked.

"Yeah." I was quiet, wondering if he was going to make the connection. I had marked the day on my calendar in bright pen and circled it a couple of times, but so far none of my brothers had clued in to the fact that it was my birthday we would be celebrating tonight.

"And that Juanita girl and her kid?"

"Juanita and Kent will be there, too."

When Chip had found out I was having company, he had asked if Juanita could come, as well. I wasn't crazy about the idea.

Tracy had been involved with Kent when he started hanging around the vet clinic before school. Juanita had initially been distrustful of Tracy's concern for Kent. Though she had since come to realize that Tracy wasn't trying to take Kent away from her and, in fact, hoped that Kent could be reunited with his mother once Juanita got her act together, I still had my reservations about the mix.

When I consulted Tracy she told me she was fine with it and that it was my birthday party and that I could do whatever I want. So I reluctantly had said yes. Now, from the wheedling tone in my brother's voice, he wanted a favor from me and I suspected it required setting an extra plate. "Why do you need to know?"

"Well, could we have another person come?"

I knew it. I dropped a bunch of green onions in a bag and twined a tie around it with a vicious twist of my wrist and decided to beat my brother to the punch. "Yes, James can come."

The silence was worth it. "Really?"

"Yes. Really." I couldn't fight this anymore. Encouraged by my brothers, this guy was encroaching on every corner of my life, so I may as well embrace the chaos and find a way to be in charge of it. Besides, it would only be until I moved away. I hugged the information to myself, gaining strength and comfort from it.

"Great. I'll let him know." He paused. "What is for supper?"

"Barbecued steak, baked potatoes, broccoli salad, rhubarb compote, mandarin salad and Tracy is bringing cake for dessert."

"Wow." The single word was spoken with hushed reverence usually reserved for an eight-second ride on a wild rogue bronc completed with a full dismount.

I waited a beat, wondering if the reason for all this bounty would sink in yet. But, nothing.

"It'll be good," I continued, hope flickering and dying. "Make sure you aren't late."

I hung up, finished my grocery shopping, and for once picked exactly the right checkout line to wait in and was out the door and back at home in record time. Dad was sitting at the table, reading the paper, and he looked up with a smile when I arrived. It had been a long time since I had seen my father out of his recliner or out of bed and the sight gave me hope. My world was slowly returning to its regular orbit, I thought as I unpacked the groceries.

As I washed and wrapped the potatoes I chatted with my dad and caught up on the events of the day. I didn't tell him about the interview, unsure of how he would take it. One step at a time, I thought as I put the potatoes on the barbecue.

I didn't expect him to remember my birthday. Dad always counted on Mom to do those honors. But maybe one of my brothers would.

Such are the dreams of the everyday sister.

"Who would have thought that a knock-kneed, cross-eyed, skinny girl could have turned into such a beautiful cook?" Jace said, licking the last of the icing off his fork. "Great cake, Tracy."

"Now don't praise her too much," David said, leaning back in his chair. "Remember beauty is only skin deep."

Tracy patted her cheek. "I have very thick skin."

"I can attest to that," David said resting his arm across the back of Tracy's chair. He glanced at me, his mouth quirked in the half smile that had, at one time, broken hearts all over Preston. "And I want to drink a toast to Dani." He picked up his glass and glanced around the table. "With hopes that we can share her delightful presence for many, many more years. Happy birthday."

Jace looked puzzled, Chip confused. Neil took another piece of cake. My father looked over his shoulder at the calendar. "Today?"

"It's today. The seventeenth. Same day it's

been since I was born." I shrugged away the faint hurt I felt at their lack. I was their only sister for goodness sakes.

But, I reminded myself, they were only guys—what did I expect? "Now, does anyone want some more cake? Juanita?"

"No, thank you. I'm sorry I didn't know it was your birthday." She threw Chip an angry glare, but he was too busy finishing off the last of the cake Tracy had brought to catch or even feel it. So she turned to Kent. "Honey, did you want any more?"

Kent stuck out his lower lip and blew out his breath. "Nope. I'm stuffed." He fidgeted, glancing back over his shoulder at the television that was still on, though out of consideration for our guests, Jace had muted the sound. But all through dinner I was distracted by the flickering images coming from the living room.

"Hey, sport, do you want to watch the game with us?" Jace asked, pushing himself away from the table. And before you could say "top of the ninth," Neil, Jace and my father were gravitating toward the television, sucked in by a power beyond any woman's control.

To my surprise, however, James elected to stay behind.

"This deep connection that guys have with sports teams—is that genetic or learned?" I asked of no one in particular.

"Genetic," David said decisively. I could see his head angling toward the living room, as well, underlining his comment.

He was about to say something else when he frowned and looked at his beeper. He pulled out his cell phone and left the room, which lowered the remaining male portion by half. James still sat at his end of the table, chair titled back, hands folded over his stomach.

"Can I go watch television?" Kent asked.

Juanita shook her head. "I promised Adam and Emily that you would be home on time." She glanced at me, seeking my approval. I wasn't her caseworker, but I'm sure she figured I had her caseworker Oden's ear, and she was going to mind her p's and q's as long as she was around me. "We should leave in about five minutes. It will take us half an hour to get back to Kolvik."

Chip looking longingly over at his brothers who were already cheering on their team. "We better go," Chip said, dragging his attention back to Juanita. But as soon as he looked at her, he smiled and I could see that she had his complete attention. My little brother was growing up. "I don't want to get you in trouble with Emily and Adam."

Kent pouted up at his mom, his little arms crossed on the table. "I don't want to go to Emily's. I want to go home with you, Mommy."

"In a little while," Juanita said quietly, stroking his head.

"How is your new job, Juanita?" Tracy asked. "Danielle told me you're working at the nursing home in Kolvik."

Juanita glanced from Tracy to me, as if looking for a hidden agenda. I gave her an encouraging, non-threatening smile.

"I like it," Juanita said carefully. "Some of the older people make me feel sad, a lot of them are really thankful." Juanita tucked her hair behind her ears and fidgeted. "I found a place of my own already."

"That's great," I said, pleased that she was showing such initiative. Juanita was one of the happy endings that I loved to relive. A mother who used the wake-up call issued when her child was taken away from her to change her life and turn it around. When I saw how Kent's foster parents helped her along, it made me glad to have been a part of it all.

Juanita got up and started clearing the table. "Just leave it," I said. "You better get Kent home on time."

"Are you sure?" Juanita asked, looking from me to Tracy.

"It will get done," Tracy assured her. "Don't worry."

Juanita thanked me again for having her. I got a little wave from Kent, Tracy got a hug. I understood why I didn't get one. I was the social worker, just like the one that took him away from his mother.

But it was my birthday. It would have been nice to get even one small hug from one small boy. It would have been the only one I got.

Poor little me.

Juanita and Kent left with Chip and an awkward silence fell. Tracy looked from me to James, deciphering the connection, and she was about to ask him something, when David returned.

"Sorry, but we gotta go. Bad foaling at Bredo's." He gave Tracy a sheepish grin. "I'm going to need you, my dear."

Tracy took his sheepish grin and passed it on to me. "Sorry, Dani."

"Don't worry," I said, getting up from the table, keeping my gaze diverted from the dirty dishes piled on the counter. I was going to be busy all night. "You better go."

I knew Misty Bredo, and I also knew that she'd had her eye on David from the first blink of his taillights coming into town. Even though David was married and unsusceptible to Misty's charms, Misty still liked to test the boundaries of that relationship. Better that Tracy went along to defend her territory against any incursion.

"I feel bad leaving you with all these dishes on your birthday." Tracy's gaze flicked from me to the dishes and then to James, who was also getting up. I was surprised he'd stayed as long as he had, surprised he hadn't bolted for the living room and the game.

"Don't worry, I'll help her," James said quietly.

I wasn't sure I wanted his help. Staying up until midnight and getting dishpan hands on my special day seemed preferable to navigating past James's presence in my kitchen. "I can manage."

"You can manage to have a nervous break-down," James said with a light laugh, rolling up his sleeves. "I don't mind."

"Well, I mind. I have a certain way of doing dishes."

"Yeah. Lather, rinse, repeat." Tracy raised her eyebrow toward me in a way that I could only describe as annoying. She glanced at James. "Just make sure that you don't put the wooden-handled steak knives in the dishwasher."

I tried to give Tracy a discreet glare, but James stood beside her, facing me so all I could do was try for a sudden flare of my nostrils and an unattractive widening of my eyes.

Tracy's faint wink told me that she read me loud and clear but that she didn't care. Some friend.

Then they were gone and James and I were alone in the kitchen. "So why don't you go and watch the game with my brothers," I said, projecting reasonable tones. "I appreci-ate the offer, but I'll be okay."

He laughed. "Nice try." He ignored me and stacked the empty dishes on the table on each other, dropping the cutlery in the empty water pitcher. He knew what he was doing.

I sighed loudly, to let him know that I wasn't giving in gracefully. He made me feel uncomfortable on many levels. And working with him in such close proximity was only increasing the discomfort level.

So I started stuffing leftovers into containers and stuffing the containers into the refrigerator, all the while trying to ignore James's very real presence as he scraped and rinsed and loaded dishes into the dishwasher. He said nothing, so I said nothing, but through the clink and thunk of dishes I was fully aware of his presence.

Ten minutes later I had filled the last plastic container, scraped out the last pot and put away the last piece of cake for my brothers to eat later. I had nothing else to do but wash the pots and whatever didn't fit in the dishwasher. Which meant working beside James.

I chanced a glance over my shoulder and was thrown off my stride to see James looking at me, a smile hovering over his well-shaped mouth. The dishwasher was almost full and I was surprised to see so few dishes were left on the counter. "You seem to know what you're doing," I said, in a feeble effort to cover up the sudden flush in my face at his attention.

"I've loaded a few dishwashers in my time," he said, picking up another plate and slipping it into the lower tray. "I hate doing dishes so much I make sure I pack it as full as I can."

"I'm impressed. Looks like we'll only have to wash bowls and pots."

James sucked in his lower lip, holding his hands over the dishwasher as if he were a movie director framing a shot. "If I use the top tier of the lower rack for glasses, I might be able to put one of the medium bowls in the upper rack. Depending of course on the weight of the glasses and circumference of same. Donelli's theorem could come into play here."

"It's always an inspiration to watch a master at work. But what is Donelli's theorem?"

"Friend of mine. Gord Donelli. Not too bright, but a master at loading the dishwasher. His theorem was 'if there is no room, make room.' An elegant concept if properly applied."

He rearranged the dishes and, as he promised, the bowl fit. He closed the door, studied the controls and pushed the right buttons. "So. Now what, birthday girl?"

"Pots and bowls. But you've done enough. Go join my brothers."

He tilted me a mocking smile. "And leave a woman in the kitchen to do the dishes on her birthday? Recipe for disaster."

I couldn't stop my smile. "You seem to be the only one around here that acknowledges this special day."

James glanced over at my brothers, who were cheering on their team in a way that could only be described as silly. He turned back to me and shrugged. "Did you tell them?"

"I had it marked on the calendar." I filled the sink with warm water and squirted some dish-washing soap in it, watching the bubbles form.

"But did you warm them up to the event, so to speak?" He grabbed a tea towel and snapped it once, guy style.

"They've known all my life what day my birthday is. I can't see how reminding them now will make a difference." I dropped a set of bowls into the sink.

"Because they're guys, as I hear you're fond of saying," James said, picking up a bowl I had washed and drying it. "Birthdays aren't an opportunity to score points as much as they are an event that doesn't show up on a guy's radar unless you have an early warning system in place. We need to be told."

James gave a half-hearted shrug. He seemed uncomfortable defending my brothers to me.

I scrubbed another bowl. "But that ruins the spontaneity. I like to be surprised."

"Have you ever been? Surprised, that is?"

I scraped at a caked-on piece of potato on the last bowl and shrugged. "Not really. They keep forgetting."

"So what would you sooner have? Spontaneous nothing, or planned presents?"

"I guess I'd like to think that I'm important enough to them that they want to find out what makes me happy. Then do it." I glanced over at them again. "I don't think they really care."

"They might not know exactly what makes you happy, but they do want to see you happy," James said quietly. "And I think you are important to them."

I could see that he was firmly in my brothers' corner, which, of course, he had to be. Partners in crime and all.

"You need to be clear with them, is all," he said.

"Oh, I've tried, trust me."

"Have you? When your brothers talk about you, they give me the idea that you're tough, strong and easygoing all wrapped in one attractive bundle. I never get the idea that you make demands on them."

"Of course I have. They simply prefer not to listen. And I'm not really that tough."

James frowned. "That's interesting. They make it sound like you could help with branding, break a horse, fix a motor and then go and make biscuits for lunch."

I snorted. "That was my mother. I only helped on the farm because I had no choice. I was always more into manicures and frills, but they don't seem to remember that."

"Really?"

"Really. I spent most of my life doing what they wanted and working around them. They've never had to do the same for me." Okay, birthday girl, enough whining. I don't know why I spilled all this in front of James.

"They're good guys and they really care about you." James defense of my brothers was both interesting and disconcerting.

"I suppose they do," I said. I washed the last pot and set it on the drying rack. James dried it, his eyes on me. I looked back, holding his gaze as I leaned back against the counter. Much as I fought his appeal I had to admit I was curious about him. "And how did you meet my brothers, whom you so obviously admire?"

James wiped the last pot and set it on the counter beside him. "I was new in town. My truck needed work. Someone recommended the place where Chip and Neil work. The rest, as you know, is history."

"And what brought you to Preston? It's hardly the hub of any activity other than farming and logging."

"I used to work in the oil patch. Contractor. Had a slew of equipment and a bunch of guys working for me but I got tired of the hours and the stress so I sold out and decided to find a small town that I liked. We had done some work north of here a few years ago and I remembered the place, so I came back." He folded up the towel and draped it over the drying rack.

Another surprise.

"What do you plan on doing here?"

He folded his arms over his chest, a purely masculine gesture, especially considering the breadth of his chest and the play of muscles in his arms. "Open a knitting shop," he said without changing expression.

I stifled my humor and played along. "Of

course. A man who can master the stockinet stitch pretty much has his pick of women. I imagine you'll be teaching tatting, as well."

"Silly girl, that's for later. You need a good quality cotton for tatting. For now, I'm focusing on the complexities of yarn."

I held his hazel eyes. "And you've just spun a good yarn."

"The lady has a point," he said with a wink and another smile. He didn't look away and the moment lengthened. I vaguely heard my brothers' cheer but James's eyes didn't even flicker toward the living room. It was as if he was completely focused on me.

As I held his gaze an echo of the attraction I had felt for the pre-unmasking James quivered through me and as his smile deepened. I sensed he felt it, too.

He pushed away from the counter the same time I did, bringing us closer to each other. I could catch the vague scent of laundry soap, the tang of his aftershave.

Then his hand touched my face, and cupped my cheek. The rough tips of his finger gently brushed back and forth in a hypnotic gesture.

I swallowed a sudden flutter of panic as he stepped closer. I could feel the warmth of his hand, see the faint beating of his pulse in his neck, catch the gold flecks in his hazel eyes.

He was going to kiss me and I wanted him to. I might even get my first birthday hug of the day, I thought as his hand drifted down to my shoulder, gently pulled me closer.

Then the doorbell sent out an insistent summons. I blinked and reason intruded.

Was I crazy? Fool me once, shame on you. Fool me twice…

I had plans and I had to see them through. It was sheer loneliness that had me momentarily beguiled by this handsome man. That and the fact that at one time I had been attracted to him. Well, to his alter ego. Doing the dishes hadn't hurt his cause, either.

The doorbell rang again, and I twisted away, hurrying to answer it.

A young woman stood on the step, the outside light casting her face into shadow, but from first glance she looked to be about eighteen. She wore a denim jacket, skin-tight blue jeans, a low scooped T-shirt and an insolent grin, as if I was supposed to know her.

She had a large suitcase parked beside her, a purse over one arm, and on her other hip, a one-year-old girl.

The young woman's deep blue eyes, framed by high, plucked brows, swept over me. "I heard you can help me." She tossed her long auburn hair back from her face, adjusting the child, who sat passively on her hip.

My mind swept back over cases trying to place her or the little girl, but I came up blank on both counts.

"I'm sorry, I don't know who you are."

"But James does." She looked past me and smiled, hitching the little girl higher up on her hip. "Hey, honey. I'm home."

Chapter Seven

I stared at the young woman as her words sunk in. Honey? Home? I turned to James, who stood behind me with his mouth open, his eyes looking like a deer caught in the glare of headlights.

"Robin." The single word came out as if he had been punched in the stomach.

Anger flashed through me at the little tableau. I had been moments away from making a colossal fool of myself, but had now been literally saved by the bell. I wanted to leave, but was hemmed in by James's little girlfriend—or wife or whatever—and her daughter in front of me, and the piker himself behind me.

"Hey, James. Meet Sherry." Robin picked

up her little girl's hand and made her wave it. "Sherry, say hi to Uncle James."

Uncle James?

My mind did a 180-degree turn. The child wasn't his. But then...

"Danielle, I'd like you to meet my sister, Robin. Robin, this is Danielle."

"Hey," Robin said, tipping her chin toward me in, what I guessed, was a type of greeting. She clasped her child closer, shifting her weight as the tired little girl drooped against her mother.

Sister. Robin was his sister. Uncle wasn't an evasive nickname that many single mothers give their live-in boyfriends. Sherry was James's actual niece.

As the pieces fell into place I felt a little bit foolish. Judge not...

I stepped back to invite Robin in and ran right into James. He caught me by the shoulders to steady me. His hands lingered a moment before he lowered them.

Robin's eyes narrowed as she looked from me to him and back again and I recognized the look of a proprietary sister. Not that I used it much myself of late, but at one time, when Jace or Neil would bring a girl home,

I would try it on. They never caught on. Men never did, but then the look wasn't for them. It was for the other woman.

Not that I was "other woman" material, I wanted to hastily assure her. James wasn't my type. At all.

You didn't seem to think that a moment ago.

Brain freeze. Birthday blues. All of the above.

"Would you like to come in?" I asked, looking at Sherry. The child was yawning and rubbing her red eyes. Her hair hung in damp curls around her rosy face. I didn't have much in the way of baby food but I could find something for the poor child.

"No. I want to get Sherry to bed." Robin shook her head, not looking at me. "I didn't see your truck," she said to James. "Did you get another one?"

"No. I live on the yard here," James said.

Another piercing look shot my way. I wanted to put my hands up in a gesture of surrender. Not my idea.

"How did you get here?" James asked.

Robin held up her thumb and grinned at us. "Return trip ticket."

She was hitchhiking with a baby? Was she insane?

"Are you nuts?" James pushed past me, towering over his sister, his eyes wide with indignation, his words echoing my thoughts. "You don't hitchhike with a baby."

Robin tilted her shoulder up in a casual shrug. "How else was I supposed to get here?"

James glanced at me as if seeking help with how to deal with this new twist in his life. What did I know about young sisters who show up on doorsteps with a baby? I dealt with young mothers who tried to leave theirs on doorsteps. So I gave him my "I don't know" look and underlined it with a shrug.

Though I had to admit, it was interesting to see how flustered a tall, well-built man could get when faced with the tiniest of human beings.

"And how did you find me?" he asked, running his hands through his hair in a gesture of frustration.

"Erwin, the guy you used to work with, told me." Robin shifted the little girl again. "But, hello? Baby? Tired? We need to go."

"Okay. Give me a minute to figure out what to do." Another helpless glance my way.

"I don't imagine you have a crib or anything Sherry could sleep in?"

While James had been dealing with this new twist to his life, I had been thinking about where this child would lay her tired head. "You know, there might be an old crib in the attic of your house," I said, trying to remember. "When we moved in here, Mom and Dad didn't clean everything out of the old house. It might be in pieces, if it is though."

"That would be great." He blew out a sigh and dragged his hand over his face, then angled me a half smile. "Thanks for dinner and, well, happy birthday." He waited a beat.

Was I supposed to do something? Thank him for coming? Kiss him goodbye? Knit booties for Sherry?

"Thanks," I said. Brevity was the soul of wit and of goodbyes.

"Okay, then," he said slowly. "I'll be gone. See ya."

And then he was. Gone.

I couldn't hear what they were saying as they walked away, but the tone of his voice carried quite well.

Not hard to hear that he was very, very angry.

And me? I was very, very curious.

* * *

"I have to say I'm quite impressed with your credentials." The man sitting across the desk from me gave me an encouraging smile. Dan Crittenden was my potential boss, depending on how the interview went.

Beside me was Les Steglund, a potential fellow employee who Dan had asked to sit in on the interview, as well. Apparently, Les was being groomed for an executive position in the company.

Though the company was registered as a non-profit, its offices and appointments were impressive.

I tried not to feel intimidated by either the men or the surroundings. So far the best way to accomplish that seemed to be imagining each of these well-groomed men with grease on their hands and billed caps on their heads.

It was quite a stretch considering they each wore suits tailored to the nth degree. But it was the only way I could feel in charge.

Dan had my papers laid out in a neat fan on his wide mahogany desk. From the floor-to-ceiling windows behind him the early morning light poured in, for now muted by gauzy curtains.

Cloth curtains. In an office.

The office was on the tenth floor of a building that overlooked the river valley that was edged with parks and treed areas. Downtown, and yet with such a beautiful view. I could get used to this, I thought, settling back in my leather chair.

I'd managed to get the morning off to drive down here for this interview, though I had to promise Casey I would make up for it by working extra this afternoon and evening, which meant I had to get my brothers to make sure Dad had supper tonight.

Supper.

Panic clutched my chest. In my excitement to get here I had forgotten to remind my brothers to feed my father. I needed to write it down, but scribbling a note on my hand while I was in an important interview wouldn't look like I was focused on the here and now.

And here and now, I wanted this interview to go well.

"Your current job is the first one you got right out of college?" Dan was asking me, pulling me back to the job at hand.

"Yes. It was an opportunity to stay with my

family for a while." Only I hadn't planned on the "a while" lasting this long.

"I noticed you had Professor Croft for sociology at the U of A," Les was saying. His smile blazed out at me, white teeth against tanned skin. Les was easy to look at. In spite of the fact that he was sitting beside me I could see that he was tall. Blond hair. Blue eyes. Suit. Tie. Silk tie. Very nicely put together.

"Did you attend U of A, as well?" I asked Les, jumping on this small connection. Dan and Les were interviewing four other candidates for this job and I needed to stand out.

"Yes. Spent some of my best years there." Another smile.

"Your overall performance review is also excellent," Dan was saying and I looked back at him. "How do you feel about your current job?" he asked me.

My current job and my current boss are the reason I'm here.

But to my credit I went with, "I enjoy the challenges my job gives me."

I mentally cringed at the rehearsed line. Tracy had tried to convince me to go for spontaneous, but I was so nervous about getting this job that I didn't trust what would come spilling out of my mouth if I ventured into unknown terrain. I could conceivably start by talking about my job and end up discussing the advantages of synthetic over regular engine oil. So I had spent the two hours of the drive down here wisely. Rehearsing. "Much as I enjoy the challenges," I continued, "I feel like I'm ready to try something else."

Now wasn't that nice and bland. If I wanted my interview to stand out, I wasn't exactly surging to my feet here.

Dan nodded, no expression on his face. "I am a little concerned about your lack of experience in the adoption field, however," he said. "How do you think that lack would hinder you in this job?"

Hinder me? Now he wanted me to underline my shortcomings?

This interview was slowly falling away from me and we had barely gotten started.

Please, Lord, help me concentrate, I prayed as I clasped and unclasped my hands in my lap as my thoughts skittered around, gathering useless information. *I don't want to end up living with my brothers until I'm eighty-five. I really want this job.*

I took a deep, calming breath, opened my hands and looked Dan straight in the eye. "I prefer to look at what I can bring to this job," I said quietly. "In my work I have dealt with children who have been taken away from their parents at various ages and stages of their lives. Regardless of how poorly these children have been treated, I've seen strong parent/child bonds and have come to recognize how powerful that relationship can be. What I believe I can do for any adoptive parent is prepare them for the reality of that bond. I am aware that your agency's track record includes a high placement of children under the age of one as well as the overseas adoptions of infants. This adds a cultural context to the adoption that can, at times, be as strong and add as much complexity to the potential relationship as the biological connection children have with their natural parents." Listen to me. I was on a roll and I knew that sooner or later I should be stopping or Dan and Les were going to fall asleep, but the words spilled out of my mouth in one unbroken stream. "I believe that I can not only help place children with parents, but be a support to them after the fact. I also believe that this component is lacking in your organization and if I were to be hired, I would like to see this support network put in place for the sake of the adoptive parents. They need to have ongoing care and consideration. I mean, you're charging them an arm and a leg to get them a baby and I think they could use a little more bang for their buck."

Ouch.

Had I really said "bang for their buck" in a professional setting? Had I seriously used the phrase "arm and a leg" when referring to adopting babies in an interview for a job I desperately wanted?

Well. How to make your interview stand out. Criticize the company you're going to be working for and use colloquialisms more suited to dealing with a cattle auction.

Dan's smile slipped a little. Not a good sign. But I heard a stifled chuckle from Les beside me. For a moment I wished the men were switched around. Les seemed more approachable.

Dan looked at my papers again. His frown was not a positive. He stroked his chin with one finger. "That's interesting."

If there's one word that women can

decipher it is the ubiquitous "interesting." Replace that with "I've got a radical nutcase on my hands and how can I get rid of her?" and I think I nailed that translation. Now the only thing left to do was say goodbye and make a graceful exit.

"And a good point." He nodded lightly, absorbing my flood of information, tapping his gold pen on his blotter. "I really appreciate the input I've received from you."

I had slipped forward, ready to get up, but when my tired brain caught the word "appreciate" I settled back in my chair.

"Tell us a bit more about some of the work you've done," Les said, leaning forward.

Obviously the interview was still a work in progress.

We chatted for another half an hour. I found out more about the job. I would have my own office and, possibly a secretary. It all sounded so very civilized.

Kind of tame.

I pushed down the ungrateful thought. Tame is why I took this job. I worked with the Beast and was tired of wild and untamed.

The interview moved from my work to my life and somehow I ended up telling them about my brothers, about my life in Preston and how I wanted to leave.

Les laughed in the right places and seemed genuinely interested in what I was telling him. Dan simply sat back, commenting now and then.

Of the two, Les was easier to talk to. Of course, it helped that he was good-looking, as well. Good-looking in a refined and cultured way that appealed to the part of me that was tired of grease and dirt on my men.

His hands were immaculate, his nails clean and neatly cut. His hair was artfully tousled and held in place with gel. Just like James's had been the first time I saw him.

After a while, I saw Dan discreetly glance at his watch and I knew my time was up.

I got to my feet and slung my purse over my shoulder. "Thank you for taking the time to see me," I said, looking at Dan, then Les. "I appreciate it."

"No. I should thank you for an interesting and lively interview," Dan said, getting up. "You will be notified if you receive the job. Les will show you out."

That sounded good to me.

I followed Les out the door and as he shut it, I let out my breath.

"Don't worry," Les said. "You did great." His blue eyes held mine as he smiled again. "This may sound presumptuous, but would you have time for a cup of coffee? There's a place around the corner that I go to quite often."

I thought of Casey and the work waiting for me. But Les's blue eyes, his warm smile and, yes, his suit, brushed reason and practicality aside. Shallow, maybe, but I was ready to spend some time with a man.

"That would be lovely," I said. "But I need to put money in the parking meter."

Ten minutes later I was balanced on a tiny chair, a cappuccino perched on a table not much larger than a dinner plate. I guessed the savings on the tables paid for the leather couches, which were occupied.

Les sat across from me looking very much at ease as he sipped his grande latte. Jazz music played in the background while around me I heard snatches of conversation covering topics from IPO's to the advantages of full grain leather car seats. Not a word about grain futures or internal combustion engines. I could get used to this, I thought with a sigh.

"Tell me about your family, Danielle," Les said, giving me another brilliant smile. "I'd like to know more about you."

I took a careful sip of coffee as I tried to imagine my brothers with this man. The picture just wouldn't gel. But I forged ahead. "I have three brothers. Two older, one younger. My father is a retired farmer."

I mentally kicked myself. Agribusinessman, or even rancher, would have had a nicer ring, but Dad never cottoned to that kind of talk. He was proud to be a farmer. No need to pussyfoot around that with fancy definitions, he always said.

"So you got to grow up in the great outdoors with three brothers." His smile made me feel a little less hick-like. "I'm sure they doted on you."

"My brothers?" I thought of the time I'd played catch with Neil. He'd graciously let me borrow his glove. But when I missed a catch and the hard ball landed squarely on my nose, Neil hurried to my side more concerned for his glove than my bleeding face. "They're not so much with the doting. What about you and your family?"

"My father is a corporate lawyer. My

mother works for the Museum of Fine Arts in Toronto. I have one brother. A surgeon at The Hospital for Sick Children in Toronto."

Right. I took a sip of coffee, feeling genetically surpassed. Mechanic, welder and farmer just didn't stack up to those qualifications.

"But I didn't come here to talk about my family," Les said, putting his coffee aside and leaning his elbows on the table. And with a table this small that gesture put him close enough that I could see that his eyes were not just blue. They had shades of grey, as well. "I want to find out more about you."

"I am a social worker. I come from a small town. Not very interesting." I waved this all away as of no consequence.

To my surprise he caught my hand and gave it a gentle squeeze. His hand was large, and covered mine. His fingernails were neatly manicured. Not a speck of grease or dirt anywhere. "Don't talk like that," he said, lowering his voice intimately. "You are a fascinating person. I'd like to get to know you better."

My heart caught in my throat as he held my hand a fraction of a second longer. No one had ever called me fascinating. I found that, well, fascinating.

"You want volume one or two?"

"I have time," he said easily. "What does your job entail?"

Entail. Good vocabulary.

So I told him. Les was the perfect audience. Laughed when he was supposed to, looked sad at the right times, shook his head at some of the more colorful characters I had to deal with.

He told me more about the job I would be doing for him and Dan. About the kind of people I would be dealing with. Mostly professionals who tried the standard adoption route, but were now willing to pay for the services that Dan's company could provide.

Our conversation ranged from work to family (his was far more erudite than mine), to holidays (Paris, Malta, Brisbane) to shopping (he actually enjoyed it). He was pleasant, easy to look at and, best of all, interested in what I had to say.

Time slipped past and suddenly, I realized we had been sitting and chatting for over an hour. I reluctantly told him I had to go.

He pulled out a business card, scribbled something on the back and handed it to me. "Here's my card. In case you have any questions."

I glanced at it then turned it over. There were two numbers written on the back.

"One of those is my cell phone number." He gave me a careful smile. "Just in case you might not get hold of me at work. And if you're ever in the city and want to connect…" He let the sentence hang and I presumed he meant that I could call him.

"Thank you." I slipped the card in my purse. I did want to connect. I did want to get to know him better.

"It was nice meeting you, Danielle," Les said. "And please, don't hesitate to call." He escorted me out of the shop, and on the street we parted ways. I watched him go then I started walking. I stopped then I tried to get my bearings. People hurried past me, each intent on what they had to do. Cars whizzed, busses zoomed. So very metropolitan, I thought, trying to imagine myself strolling so confidently through the downtown streets, knowing exactly which bistro to drink coffee at, the best places to eat.

Where to live.

For now my mission was to remember where I parked my car. I strode importantly down the street, turned left at the first avenue, crossed it, paused and then strode importantly back to where I started from as I finally remembered.

I got back in time to see a parking meter person attach a piece of paper to my windshield. Puzzled, I glanced at my watch. I was a whopping two minutes past the expired time.

Not a speck of grace was granted, I thought as I plucked the piece of paper from my windshield wiper feeling like a criminal. I got in the car, stuffed the ticket into my briefcase and paused a moment.

This is what you want, I thought as I stared straight ahead at the canyon of buildings ahead of me, traffic pouring through it, three wide going each way.

I started my car then pulled out into traffic, barely avoided turning down a one-way street, missed my street, almost hit a pedestrian, ran a yellow light and then ran into construction.

After an hour of stopping, waiting, inching forward, then waiting again, I burst through the log-jam of traffic, made my way out of the city and I was back on the highway with open fields on both sides of me. Only then did I finally released the white-knuckle grip on the steering wheel.

A tiny niggle of doubt wormed its way through my mind with each mile I drove away from the city, with each minute between now and the interview I'd just had, as well as the pleasant hour I'd spent with Les.

Are you sure this is what you want? Working in such an organized office, dealing with people who can afford to shop for their babies?

I suppose it would take time. I could get used to living in the city. To working normal hours.

Couldn't I?

I shelved my doubts, then did what any self-respecting North American woman would do in the situation. I picked up my phone and called my best friend.

"So?" Tracy demanded as soon as she picked up the phone. "How did it go?"

"I didn't talk anyone's ear off and I made sure to nod in the right places. I even had a coffee with a potential fellow male employee." I smiled then, thinking of Les.

"Don't tell me. A real man."

"A real man. The kind that holds your chair when you sit down at a restaurant and makes eye contact when you're talking to him. And I don't think any bets with my brother were involved this time."

"Speaking of food, sorry I couldn't stay to help with the dishes the other night. Did it take long?"

"Not really. James helped me."

"Really?" Tracy's pause was rife with unspoken meaning.

"Really."

"He seems like a decent guy," Tracy continued, ignoring my slightly sarcastic snort. "I didn't know he was such a looker. From the way you were talking he was two steps away from wearing a paper bag on his head."

"One step, actually." But even as I spoke, a sliver of doubt pierced my smug arguments. I remembered too well how I felt around him.

"Oh, get past the bet thing already," Tracy said. "He's going to be living right under your nose, girlfriend."

"I don't think I need to get past anything," I said with a disappointed pout. Tracy was supposed to be on my side. Why was she defending him? "Besides, his little sister stopped by that same night with a baby on her hip, so I think he'll be too busy to cause any more trouble."

"A baby? I'm sure your brothers didn't count on that when they rented the house out to him."

"Not hardly." I switched lanes to get past a tractor-trailer unit chugging up a long hill. "And I'm sure it will put a damper on whatever it is James hopes to do here in Preston."

"And what is that?"

"Who knows? He told me he was opening a knitting shop. But enough about James. I prefer to discuss Les."

We talked for a few more miles and when I had sufficiently covered all the nuances of the interview and of the semidate, and Tracy had assured me enough times that I had done well, we said goodbye.

I turned on the radio to my favorite station and relaxed against the seat, enjoying the open highway, the sun shining in my car and the fact that I'd had an interesting interview and had met an interesting man. It had been a good morning and was promising to be a good day.

It was also lunchtime and my stomach grumbled as I passed the Preston Inn. Should

I go in? I had already used up an entire morning's worth of Casey's goodwill.

Why not? I cranked the steering wheel at the last moment. I was probably already in Casey's bad books. Might as well face him on a full stomach.

And there was James, standing at the cashier paying for his lunch.

I didn't like the way my heart jumped. I was half hoping I could slip past him, but that would be rude. As Tracy reminded me I had to get past our somewhat shaky start. And, I reminded myself, he had helped me with my birthday dishes.

"Hello, James," I said.

James's head came up with a snap, then when he saw me, his mouth slipped easily into a smile.

And what annoyed me was the way my heart gave that funny little jump again when he did that.

Think of Les, I told myself. Think about the man, not the guy.

"Hey, yourself." He slipped his wallet into the back pocket of his blue jeans. He wore a suede jacket over a T-shirt today, no product in his soft and shining hair, and again I wondered what he kept busy with all day. He didn't seem to be working too hard on finding other employment or much of anything other than lunching in Preston.

Maybe he was some kind of spy. Or maybe he really was starting up a knitting shop.

"Your boss let you off your leash long enough to let you have lunch?" he asked.

"I am on my way back from the city. I had an interview for a job there." And why did I feel like I had to tell him that?

"Really?" He pulled his mouth down at the sides, like he didn't quite approve. "I don't see you as a city type."

I was crushed. I thought I had a certain savoir faire that easily translated into city girl. I wondered if he could see me with Les Steglund, but wasn't about to put that question to him. "And how is Robin doing?" I asked instead.

James caught his lower lip between his teeth and shook his head. "She just got out of a bad relationship. Robin has her own problems and I know I can't fix them. I wish she wouldn't come running to me all the time."

"I know what you mean."

James gave me an odd look. "Maybe you

do, at that," he said. He hesitated a moment, as if he wanted to say something else. Then tossed me a wave and left.

I watched him go, feeling as if the day had shifted again.

Six hours later I parked my car behind Jace's truck on the yard and leaned my head back with a sigh. What a lousy day.

All afternoon Casey had been doing his best mini-dictator imitation—making me redo a custody agreement, rewrite an assessment—his small revenge for my absence this morning and, I supposed, my interview. I had phoned my brothers and while I was typing, ignoring Casey's hovering presence and trying to make sense of his notes, I walked Jace through the onerous and complicated process of heating up leftovers for supper.

Thankfully, Dad could at least feed himself, otherwise who knows how that scenario would have played out.

Then, after all those unreasonable demands on my sanity that threatened my very salvation, Casey sent me to do a home-study on a family that wanted to be foster parents, but were hostile about the steps they had to go

through. I used up every drop of good nature
and charm to convince them that the training
they were going to take was for their own
good. And that, yes, they had a lot of experience because they raised five children, but
foster children required a different tack and
other skills.

I got the feeling they didn't believe me, but
I knew that when they had to deal with their
first six-year-old runaway, or eight-year-old
arsonist, they'd thank me.

That was my life these days. Always in the
wrong place at the right time.

So now it was eight o'clock. I was
starving and hoped that Neil wouldn't find
the last piece of cake I had hidden in the last
place my brothers would look—the vegetable drawer.

I stepped out of the car, my head feeling as
if it were going to float off my body, when I
heard the unmistakable sound of a baby crying.

Loud. And coming from James's home.

It's not your problem, I assured myself as I
closed the door and hefted my briefcase over
my arm. Robin seems like a capable person.
She hitchhiked here, didn't she? With a baby.

But the crying didn't stop. I heard a deep

voice singing some off-key version of a nursery rhyme. James?

Curious, I walked down the driveway toward his house and saw him walking past the window, holding the baby.

He stopped, looked out the window and saw me. He looked terrified.

Chapter Eight

I hurried to the house and yanked open the door, my heart pounding. What could have happened? Did I need to call an ambulance? How was my infant CPR? Rusty. Would I be of any help?

James met me at the door, holding out a screaming, flailing infant.

"Please. Help me," James begged, his voice haggard as he shoved his niece at me. "I can't make her stop."

I glanced at him, then at the child who was now twisting and squirming in my arms, her cries cutting like a serrated knife.

Other than the beet-red face and the tears pouring from her scrunched up eyes, she seemed healthy enough.

"Did you feed her?" I yelled, letting my briefcase slip off my arm as I tried to hold her with the other.

"I tried. She wouldn't drink her bottle. Wouldn't eat her porridge or whatever you call that slop," James shouted, as he ran his hands through his hair in a gesture of defeat. "Nothing helped."

"Where's Robin?"

"Don't know. I came home and this kid was crying and she's heading out the door."

I gave up trying to converse with James over the wails of this obviously distressed child. Instead I tried to cuddle her as I walked slowly around James's living room. It was like trying to hold a hysterical eel. She kicked, she thrashed, she lunged from side to side.

"Diapers? Do you have any clean diapers?" I called out to James.

He frowned, not comprehending what I was talking about.

"Did Robin have a big bag with stuff for the baby in it?" I yelled.

He nodded and ran into another room and returned with a diaper bag. He dropped it on the floor, ripped it open and started pulling clothes out, tossing them behind him in a mad effort to find some diapers.

I laid Sherry on the floor, anchoring her twisting body with one hand on her stomach as I liberated the diaper bag from James. I quickly found what I needed, then glanced at the floor. Carpet.

The couch beside me was leather. What to do?

My hand hovered over the tabs of the diaper. Who knew what mysteries awaited me once I opened things up.

Oh, well. Nothing for it. This carpet had seen its share of substances and I didn't want to take any chances with James's couch. So I ripped off her diaper, then almost gagged as a horrible, sour smell assaulted me. Just as I suspected. The little girl's bottom was red and raw.

I handed James a face cloth that he had yanked out of the bag and tossed in my vicinity. "Wet this with warm water."

Poor little Sherry arched her back and lifted her bottom clear off the smelly diaper. She held that position until James returned with the face cloth and I could nicely get at all parts that showed and remove the offending diaper. I folded it up one-handed.

"Can you get rid of that?" I asked.

James pulled a face, then picked it up between thumb and forefinger, allowing as little of his flesh to come into contact with it as possible.

"Is this considered hazardous waste?" he asked.

"Do with it what you think best," was all I could advise.

In a matter of minutes Sherry was cleaned up, lotion was smeared and her cries were subsiding from wails into half-hearted little hiccups. I took off the rest of her clothes, now damp with her sweat, and put on a clean, dry terry cloth footie sleeper, tucking her arms and legs in. As I snapped it up, she drew in a quavering breath. Then, in spite of the tears that still sparkled on her long eyelashes, she granted me an open-mouthed grin, two little pearls of teeth glinting back at me.

James fell back against the couch that had been spared the indignity of having a dirty diaper on it and sighed heavily. "I wouldn't have thought of that. I mean, I didn't smell a thing."

"They put so much scent in these disposable diapers, it's hard to know what's really in them." I picked Sherry up and cuddled her close, feeling sorry for the poor little mite. "Hey, little thing. You couldn't tell us what was wrong could you?" I was using my baby voice to talk to her. As if pursing my lips and raising my tone an octave would magically penetrate her tiny brain and make a connection. She drew in a quavering breath and smiled again. She was adorable. How could Robin leave her like this?

James rubbed his temples with his fingers as he leaned back against the couch. "You, my dear, are a lifesaver. I didn't know what to do. I come home and there's Robin holding Sherry, and she shoves the baby in my arms and tells me she's leaving, and then she's gone and Sherry starts crying, and no matter what I do I can't get her to stop and I'm all ticked at my sister who's left me in the lurch. Again."

I cuddled little Sherry close, looking at James, amazed at his verbal spill. "And here I thought you were the strong, silent type."

He laughed, rolling his neck and drawing in a long, slow breath. "Strong maybe, but not too silent." He lifted his head, his smile slowly fading away. "Seriously, thanks a ton. I didn't know what to do with that little thing."

"That little thing" now lay quietly in my arms, her sniffs slowly subsiding. She grew warm and heavy in my arms and I guessed she was falling asleep. My legs were cramping up, but I didn't dare get up. The only chair I could lean against sat at right angles to James. I didn't have a choice, so I moved closer to give my tired back some ease.

"Why hadn't you seen Sherry before?" I asked, as I settled into this new place, too close to James, but better for my back than sitting in the middle of the floor.

James laughed, but it wasn't a funny laugh. More like a snort of disgust. "After I found out she was pregnant, Robin took off and I didn't get to hear from her, much less see her until now. She won't tell me who the father is and won't make any plans." James pulled his hands over his face, his callused hands rasping against his whiskers. Obviously not the hands of a knitter. "I didn't even know if she had a boy or girl until Robin showed up at your house. Which I apologize for. I don't know how she found me."

"You're new. People talk, ask questions. In no time at all they've got you pegged and know where you live." I rubbed my chin absently over Sherry's feather-soft curls. "Though I think most people will be surprised when you open your wool shop."

James laughed, then rested his wrists on his upraised knees, letting his hands dangle. "I can knit two, purl three with the best of them." James yawned a jaw-cracking yawn and rubbed the top of his head, making his hair look like a mouse's nest. A kind of attractive mouse's nest, I had to admit. He rolled his head in my direction. "So, since I saw you at lunchtime, how was the rest of your day?"

"Mine?"

"Yeah. I already know how Sherry's went." His half smile balanced out the faintly bitter tone.

"The usual. Casey pushing me to do more than most humans are capable of and me trying to do it." I shrugged.

"Ah, a nurturer." His half smile morphed into a sly grin.

I held up a warning hand. "Don't stick me in a box."

"I see how you take care of your brothers. I've never seen such a devoted sister. It's admirable in one way."

"It's not about being a devoted sister, it's

pure survival. The house would be a disaster if I didn't maintain control."

"What would happen if you didn't clean and cook and keep your brothers organized?" He picked up a tiny face cloth that he had tossed out of the diaper bag and folded it up slowly.

I snorted to myself. "Their lives would fall apart."

He gave me a knowing look. "I wasn't talking about *their* lives."

Walked right into that one. I looked down at Sherry. Her lashes fanned her cheeks, her button mouth was partly open—a line of glistening drool pooling on the lapel of my suit jacket.

"Do you want me to take her?" James asked, moving closer.

I hesitated, surprised at my reluctance to let her go.

The little body in my arms brought out fuzzy, warm maternal feelings in me I didn't even know I had. Most of my baby handling would fall under the extreme-babysitting category. Taking children away from neglectful parents in highly stressful situations. Handling dirty, crying children who hated me for what I was doing to them.

Hardly moments for adorable cuddling time, like now.

But Sherry needed to go to bed and I needed to go home. The day had been a mixture of hope and depression. Hope for a new job and depression that my old life wouldn't be as easy to shuck off as I thought.

I shifted Sherry to hand her over. She stiffened, drew in a quick breath and let out a halfhearted whimper as her head came up.

I willed her to relax and then she slowly slumped back into sleeping mode. "Maybe better wait a while," I whispered to James.

He nodded, but stayed where he was. About five inches closer to me than he had been before.

I bent closer to Sherry's warm head, inhaling her soft baby smell. Robin may be a fly-by-night mother, but Sherry's sleeper held that fresh-washed scent of laundry soap.

"So tell me why an attractive woman like you still doesn't have a steady boyfriend." James slouched against his couch. "According to your brothers you've dated enough guys."

"Men," I corrected primly. "I prefer to stay away from guys."

"I noticed." He yawned again, and blinked

slowly, his eyes taking on a languorous look. "Can't find the perfect man in Preston?"

I didn't like the challenge in his voice, or the look in his eye. "No," I said, my voice taking on a chill that came naturally around this guy. "The men that drift into this town seem to have an aversion to sticking around or working a job that doesn't require being gone half of the time." I didn't like the direction of the conversation or the way my leg was cramping up.

Hard pain stabbed me in the hip. I moved my leg.

Sherry shifted, stiffened, lifted her head and started crying. I stroked her head, and settled back against the chair sitting at right angles to James.

"Can I make you a cup of tea or coffee?" James asked.

"No, thanks." I glanced down at Sherry. "I hope this little mite settles pretty soon. I have to get home."

"I think your dad is sleeping, so he won't need you."

"I have church tomorrow."

"Your brothers go, too, don't they?"

My usual sorrow over my brothers' lack of

commitment followed on the heels of his comment. "Jace goes once in a while. Chip and Neil are still struggling with the whole 'church is for sissies' concept." I held his gaze, wondering if he would side with either Jace or my other brothers.

Then I wondered why I cared. What James thought or did not think of church shouldn't matter to me.

James simply shrugged. "I think it takes real conviction to attend church, especially these days when men—" he gave me a wry grin "—or guys, don't see a need for a relationship with God or recognize that they need a personal savior. I think the modern Church has made God so tame, guys can't relate."

"What do you mean 'tame'?"

James pulled his lower lip between his teeth, his look faraway. "When I was little, my dad would read me the Narnia books. There was one passage he emphasized again and again—the part about Aslan being a lion and not being safe. I knew it was an allegory of Christ. I thought about it lots when I was a teenager and the Church was always making Jesus out to be meek and mild. I always thought of Him as a bold, fearsome man, God in the flesh and God, well if you look at the world He created, the power and the force, God is hardly tame."

I have to confess, I was surprised. "So you do go to church?"

James looked away from me and picked up a terry face cloth that had been discarded in his mad dash for a dry diaper. "Used to. My father died when I was fifteen, so to support us, my mother started working as a waitress. I got on at the same restaurant and we ended up working a lot of Sundays." He pressed a fold in the terry cloth with one large finger. "She never talked about God anymore or about church. When I got a job on the oil rigs, I never went at all."

"And now?"

He shrugged. "I don't know. I've been gone so long, it would seem disrespectful to suddenly show up."

I didn't know if I agreed with his vision of God. I'd always thought of God as a God of love. "I think a God that can count the hairs on someone's head can remember one of his own," I said softly, surprised at this side of him. "We have church tomorrow, if you're interested in going."

He shrugged. "I'll see."

I don't know why his answer disappointed me so much. For just a moment, a tiny moment, I had caught a glimmer of a faint, hopeful possibility.

Of what? Transformation from guy to man?

"When will you hear about this city job?" James asked quietly, moving the topic of conversation to something more ordinary. Safer, I guess, than talking about God and Jesus and faith. Chip and Neil did the same whenever I brought up church or church attendance. But I was willing to discuss my future. It gave me a better kind of hope. My ticket away from Casey, my unbearable boss, and my brothers.

"I was told in about two weeks."

"You would take it?"

"Oh, yes. I need to get away from Preston, my current boss and, if I'm going to be honest, my brothers. The city seemed a logical choice."

"But you love your brothers." His voice took a faint upturn at the end of the statement adding the hint of a question.

"Of course I do. But lately 'inconsiderate' is too small a word to describe them."

"Well, it's your own fault, really."

"What?" I stared at him with a mixture of anger and disbelief at his blunt statement. "You're going to get a hernia leaping to that conclusion."

"You don't ask for their help. You let them get away with being lazy."

I let out an unladylike snort. "And isn't that a typical guy response. If women would get our act together, we could get men to do the right thing."

"Behind every good man, et cetera." He straightened then leaned forward to emphasize what he was saying. "But the reality is men need a push and if they don't get it, they think everything is fine."

"So what you're telling me is that guys can't think for themselves." My voice rose, Sherry stiffened and I bit back my next comment.

"They can think," James said, reaching over and gently turning Sherry's head so it lay more comfortably. "What women think they should think about isn't the same thing as what men like to think about."

"That's chauvinistic," I whispered, wishing he hadn't left his hand on Sherry's head, so close to my shoulder. "And confusing."

"You complain that your brothers don't do anything," he whispered back, "yet you don't ask them. How are they supposed to know? We're a results-based, problem-solving species, us men. Give us a problem and we'll solve it. If we don't think there's a problem, hey, nothing to solve and we go back into sleep mode. Like a computer."

"So like a computer, guys need to be booted up. Or just plain booted." I tried to focus on what he was saying, but half of my attention was on his hand that gently feathered Sherry's curls away from her face. Each time he did, his fingers touched my shoulder.

"Don't kid yourself, Danielle. Guys. Men. They are exactly the same animal. Just different hairstyles and clothes so you can keep them apart. Booting might be exactly the thing either of them needs at different times."

He looked directly at me, the movements of his fingers slowing. And then his hand had moved to my shoulder.

Very smooth, I thought, but didn't look away. Didn't move away. Time slowed, pulling me to a standstill—creating this momentary bubble.

I held his gaze as my stomach fluttered, my

heart beating double time in my chest. Yes, he was attractive. Yes, he appealed to me. I cleared my throat, trying to rid myself of these foolish fancies. I had other plans. Other dreams.

Preston and this guy and my brothers were not a part of it.

I cleared my throat. "You probably subscribe to the whole *Men are from Mars, Women are from Venus* concept."

He shook his head, his fingers making slow, gentle circles on my shoulder. "Nope. Men are from earth." He moved a little closer. "Women are from earth," he whispered, his face now inches from mine. "Deal with it."

My heart gave one hard thud. His breath whispered over my cheek. His face had become a blur except for the bright light of his eyes so close to mine.

He was going to kiss me, I thought, my breath growing shallow.

And I wanted him to.

Brushing away second thoughts, I moved my head to close the gap, and for the briefest of moments our lips touched, brushed each other carefully, slowly, cautiously seeking common ground. His hand tightened on my shoulder as his mouth moved closer. He kissed me again. Longer. Slower. I was melting, disappearing.

Sherry squawked.

James pulled away.

I scurried to my feet, guilt and relief and disappointment battling with each other for the upper hand. As I walked back and forth, I tried to settle my roiling thoughts.

What had I done? What was I doing?

I cuddled Sherry close, thankful for her intervention. Remember your new job.

But was it relief that made my knees so rubbery? Or something else?

Sherry squawked again and this time, instead of using her as an excuse to stick around, I handed her to her uncle, then skedaddled out of there as fast as my tired feet would take me.

Sunday morning was the usual harried affair at the Hemstead household. At midnight, Jace had decided to heat up something to eat, but had let it boil over. So before I could make myself a cup of tea, I had to hack away a thick gob of baked-on tomato soup. Chip took too long in the shower. The hot water ran out halfway through Neil's shower so I had to listen to them harping at each other all during breakfast.

Dad was feeling alternately listless and cranky. He had to go for a doctor's appointment tomorrow, and I knew that he was nervous. I felt sorry for him but listening to him complain about his boiled eggs, his lack of coffee and the medication he had to take helped me reach maximum guy absorption.

And as a counterpoint to their grumping and griping, lay the feeling that James's kiss was like a brand on my lips that my brothers were only pretending to ignore, but secretly gloating about.

I don't know why I felt guilty, but I did feel like I had been manipulated. All the while I nibbled on my toast and sipped at my tea, I grew more self-conscious over my lack of self-control while the boys made plans for another afternoon of working broncs. With James.

After eating breakfast I retreated to my bedroom before the boys would notice how my cheeks flushed each time they mentioned his name.

I put on a gospel CD, then sat in front of my makeup table. I took my time putting on my makeup, hoping against hope that maybe the boys would have cleaned up the kitchen while I was busy.

Normally, I hummed along to my favorite songs while I exfoliated, creamed, stroked on eye shadow and put on mascara, but this morning my hand shook as I worked. I kept reliving that moment in James's living room. Wondered why he did it. Why I let him. What he thought of me now.

What I thought of him.

I wasn't sure. I knew I didn't quite trust him. *Then why did you let him kiss you?*

Loneliness. The moment. A feeling of vulnerability.

His good looks.

He is a guy. And if ever you need a reminder of why you should stay away from him, this morning is a prime example. He's like your brothers. He doesn't go to church. He's a lapsed Christian.

I threw down my lipstick tube. Messed it up again. I snatched a tissue out of the box and wiped it off, then tried again.

"Dani, time to go," Jace called out from the kitchen. I stifled a sigh. Why was he nagging me about the time when he probably wasn't going himself? As I always did when I contemplated my brother's faith life, I winged a prayer heavenward. Maybe someday. I cocked my head, listening. Was that the chink of dishes being put into the dishwasher?

"Coming," I said, my momentary funk lifting. They were good boys. They had their moments, is all. I spritzed on some perfume, nodded at my reflection in the chipped mirror and left the sanctuary of my room.

My heart sunk as I saw the dishes still piled on the table, the milk still out on the counter and the crumbs from Jace's requisite five pieces of toast still littering on the floor.

My father was napping in his recliner, Chip and Neil were gone already and Jace was flipping through the newspaper, oblivious to the havoc surrounding him.

I closed my eyes and prayed a desperate prayer for patience. Were my brothers legally blind when it came to housework? With a deep sigh I started clearing the dishes and bringing them to the counter.

"Don't have time for that, sis," Jace said, looking up from the paper. "Gotta go."

I leveled him a frustrated look. "You guys couldn't even pick one dish off the table?"

Jace's face looked puzzled. "You didn't ask."

"I'm going to be in therapy until I'm eighty." I dropped the plate I had been carrying on the nearest empty spot on the counter and walked into the living room. I abruptly shifted gears, took a long slow breath, then laid a gentle hand on my dad's head. He looked up at me and smiled.

"You okay, Dad?" I asked.

He nodded. "Just want to rest, that's all."

"We'll go for a walk when we get home, okay?"

"Sure. When you get home." He gave another weak smile and then closed his eyes again. I watched him a moment longer, willing him to get better, hoping and praying that he would so if—no, make that *when*—I left, I wouldn't have to feel like I was abandoning him to the erratic care of my brothers.

"You sure you don't want to come?" I asked Jace, hoping, praying he would decide to come.

He looked at Dad, then back at me. "Thought I would stay home with him today," he said quietly.

"Okay." My disappointment mingled with a small ray of hope. At least Jace understood what Dad needed. I took a chance and pushed a little further, remembering what James had told me the other night. "Could you possibly do the dishes then while I'm gone?"

He screwed up his face in an "I doubt it" gesture. "I've got a couple of cows calving that I need to check on…."

"Whatever," I said, stalking out of the house as my all-too-familiar refrain now sang through my head.

I've got to get out of here. I've got to leave.

James's comment of the other day slid in behind my scurrying thoughts, herding them into a place I hadn't brought them before.

Was I enabling my brothers? Did I not ask enough of them? But if I didn't do what they didn't do, what would happen to my father?

Easy for James to say as he was taking care of his infant niece. Wasn't he doing the same thing with his sister?

Right. And what else was he supposed to do?

And why was I even thinking about him when I was desperately trying to plan another life?

I put on some contemporary Christian music as I drove, breathing long, slow breaths like the stress management consultant had taught us. Half an hour later, I pulled into the church parking lot.

I checked my lipstick in my rearview mirror and got out of my car. The sun warmed my shoulders, soothing away my frustration. It was a perfect spring day. Exactly the kind of day to go out for a walk. Jace was in the middle of calving and I hadn't even had a chance to check out the new babies yet. I'm sure my dad would love to go see them, too.

I flipped my purse over my shoulder, smoothed my hair back from my face and walked to the church.

"Good morning, Danielle," an older lady boomed across the foyer as the door fell shut behind me. She sailed toward me, her bright pink suit straining across her midriff, a purple-and-orange scarf tucked into the suit coat and her expression as cheerful as her outfit. "How is your father?" she asked as she gave me a hug. Mrs. Woytowich was everyone's mother, but she hadn't been around for a while. Rumor had it she'd been taking care of her daughter in Calgary, but now it appeared, she was back and in Technicolor.

"Hey, Mrs. Woytowich," I said, thankful

for her concern. "He's doing okay. Still feeling tired, though."

"He was always such a hale and hearty man. I was sorry to hear about his heart attack. That must have been so frightening for you. And you, motherless, as well." She clucked in sympathy. "Is he here today?"

"No. He's been quite listless and has been staying home a lot."

Mrs. W. patted me on the arm. "Don't you worry. You are blessed to have your three brothers. I'm sure they're a great comfort to you."

"They are," I said with forced good humor. "If your idea of comfort was three big, messy men who have never seen a piece of laundry they couldn't trip over or a dish they couldn't wash."

"Even if they don't help much, they're good boys and I know they love you." She paused a moment, as if unsure of what to say next. "I'm sure you're busy with your work, too?"

"Yes." I gave her a vague smile, wondering where this conversation was meandering to.

"Probably too busy to do a proper job of housework and such."

"I do try," I said, hoping I didn't sound defensive.

She must have caught my sniffy tone and she let loose a loud guffaw. "Oh, honey, I know what it's like to live with a houseful of men. I was trying to be subtle but guess that went out the window." She let loose with another belly laugh. "What I really wanted to say is that I know your father's health is iffy. I'd like to come and help you and your family."

"Help. How?"

"Oh, general stuff. Cleaning. Some cooking. Visiting your father." She waved her hand—a mere whiff of time for her.

I looked at her, trying to take in this potential shift in my life. "What would you charge?"

She frowned. "Charge. Don't be absurd. I'm at loose ends and a little bored. I could use the company."

"Well…let me think about it…."

"Give me a call. I'll be waiting." Mrs. W. winked at me, then called out someone's name and was off on another mission.

I wandered into church, still trying to absorb all of this. Could it be that those odds-and-ends prayers I had for a chance to move away had finally been answered? Could it be that the last hindrance to my moving to the city was whisked away by a brief conversation in the church foyer? Was she a fuchsia godsend?

Tracy and David were already seated and I slipped in beside them.

"You're looking pretty chipper." Tracy said. "Casey transfer out of Preston or something equally heartwarming?"

"Something almost as heartwarming," I said evasively. She would hardly share my enthusiasm in having the problem of my father solved so quickly.

"What are your brothers up to today?"

"Neil and Chip decided to go to Kolvik." Obviously things were moving right along in the Chip and Juanita situation. I hoped he didn't run into Steve Stinson. "Jace said he was going to stay home with Dad and check on some cows and not do the breakfast dishes," I grumbled, glancing over the bulletin.

Tracy wisely changed the subject, telling me instead about the newest plans they had decided on for the house. "David even approves, so things look like they're moving along quite well."

"I'm not that hard to please," David put in, putting the bulletin away and slipping his arm around Tracy. He gave me that crooked smile that could make so many women's hearts go pitty pat. At one time I wasn't immune, either, but I've gotten to know him too well to see him as anything else but David, a good friend and the husband of my best friend.

"Excuse me."

A deep voice beside me made me look up. And my mouth went dry.

Chapter Nine

James. Wearing a casual shirt, corduroy blazer and clean blue jeans. A perfect hybrid of the "man" who loved Schubert and the guy who loved bucking broncs. He was good, I'll give him that.

My eyes drifted to his mouth that quirked up in his now trademark smile, as if he were laughing at some interior joke. I thought of his kiss and my lips burned.

"Is this seat saved?"

"No, but I'm praying for it." Nervousness brought out my dark humor. I had hoped I wouldn't see him after last night's kiss.

"Well, I'll help things along," he said, slipping in beside me as if everything was all peachy keen between us.

Tracy nudged me and I glared at her, but she wouldn't back down. I rolled my eyes and turned to James.

James displayed courtesy and charm, but while he spoke, I couldn't keep my eyes off his mouth. I couldn't stop thinking about the kiss. How his face had softened before he moved in. How I had met him partway.

You're in church, you ninny. Get a grip.

"So what brings you to church today?" I asked, injecting into my voice a tone of nonchalance. Keep things simple and superficial. He was *not* the man for me.

"Memories of other church services," he said. "Some of the things we talked about the other night."

My heart fluttered again at his serious tone and the hint of yearning in his voice. I'd heard it the other night, as well. When he kissed me.

"And the fact that they have a free nursery," James added.

His mocking look dampened the faint warmth that his previous comment had kindled in me. "Of course," I said, feeling foolish.

I was about to turn away, but as I caught his gaze again, his sardonic smile softened. "I'm kind of kidding about the nursery," he said, his voice dropping enough to create a hint of intimacy.

Again his eyes held mine. Again I felt like I was drifting into a new, different place. His smile faded and I saw him swallow.

"Danielle…"

A crash of musical chords surrounded us as the singing group at the front started up. I jumped. James looked away.

My heart fluttered as I slowly got to my feet, my mind trying to connect to the words flashing on the screen overhead. I caught the rhythm, caught the song. But as I sang, I was intimately aware of the man beside me.

Forgive my distraction, Lord, I prayed as my eyes followed the words, trying to pull myself into worship. Into the realization that I was in God's house and worshiping Him.

I slowly was drawn into the song, but even so, I heard James's voice beside me, hesitant at first as he learned the words, then more forceful as he caught on.

Then the first few songs were done, and the worship leader was welcoming us to the service, inviting us to greet the people around us.

I took a quick breath and shook James's

hand officially welcoming him to our church service. I kept my voice cool and calm.

He looked down into my eyes and gave my hand an extra squeeze at the end. Nervy as a pickup artist in church. Which is exactly what he was.

I went through the motions of chatting briefly with the people ahead of me, behind me. Said hello to Tracy and David again, and tried to make myself concentrate on the music as the praise team started singing.

I closed my eyes to help me concentrate. I was here to be a part of a community that worshiped God. I listened to the words, let them become a part of me and slowly let myself be carried to another place, a place close to my Savior, in His presence.

By the time the pastor came to the front of the church, I was in the right frame of mind for worship.

We had a visiting minister today and he spoke on Exodus 33 when Moses was up on the mountain and he asked God to show Moses His glory.

"'I will have mercy on whom I will have mercy and I will have compassion on whom I have compassion. But you cannot see my face, for no one may see me and live,'" he said.

He continued on to the end then looked around at us and began speaking again. When he spoke of God's mercy and compassion, I felt comforted. Encouraged. I struggled each day with people who I needed to deal with compassionately, even though I didn't think they deserved it.

But then he went on to speak of God's glory. God's power. How God dealt with Job when Job dared to question Him. How God has shown time and time again that He is a God to be reckoned with, not a tame beast that we can send on errands with our prayers. How we approach a God so holy that even a glimpse of His face would kill us.

"He is a God of power and judgment," the minister said, "and we need to remember that. Because while we can be comforted by His compassion shown to us in taking on fragile human flesh, we can also be comforted to know that He conquered death. *Conquered*," the minister emphasized. "It was a battle and He won. Jesus has laid claim to this world and He is in charge."

I was taken aback by his passionate message.

I know I didn't always like to read the prophets in the Old Testament. They always seemed so harsh and, well, judgmental.

But isn't God a judge as well as a Savior? Isn't He also the King and Ruler of this earth?

I glanced sidelong at James and thought again of his memory of his father. How God isn't "safe" but He is good. These ideas shifted my ongoing perception of God. And, possibly, my perception of James.

The last chords of the last song died away and then the praise group moved into another chorus and conversation started to swell as people made their way out of church.

I waited a moment, letting the message sink in.

I turned to James, but he was already walking away, heading toward the nursery. I saw a few women's heads turn, watching him. Just as I was.

"Could you? Please?" Chip caught my hands and squeezed, giving me his best sad, puppy dog face.

"Chip, I haven't had an empty evening to myself in weeks. I was hoping to get together with Tracy." I got up from the kitchen table and tied on an apron. This time I was going to be firm. Just as James had encouraged me to. "Babysitting isn't really high on my 'want to do' list."

"But if James doesn't get anyone to watch Sherry, he can't come check out those new broncs of the Alamedas. They're supposed to be real goers. Drake Alameda wants us to break the one for riding."

I'd worked well into the evening this past Monday and Tuesday. And each night as I dragged myself home, I would look over at James's house and wonder what he was doing—how he was managing. I'd slow down, think about stopping, but each time the memory of his kiss and the thought of him in church would mingle together with the picture of him riding that wild bronc. It was altogether confusing and frustrating. And now on my first free night, Chip wanted me to nurture and help that part of James along.

"Why would I want to make it easier for James to potentially break his neck on some 'goers.'" I put sarcastic emphasis on the last word. Honestly this "wild at heart" thing was getting a bit overdone.

"He loves doing it. Besides, he's better with the horses than we are."

"Of course he would love doing it," I muttered. I don't know why it should bother me that James was no different from my brothers when it came to putting his neck on the line. Surely having the responsibility of a little baby should have tempered that very "guy" urge. I pulled out two onions from the refrigerator and started chopping them up, sniffing as the fumes overtook me.

"It would really help out if you could. I mean, it's not his fault his sister took off on him." Chip came around to the sink and leaned on the counter, trying to catch my eye.

"It's not my fault, either. Has he heard anything from Robin?"

Chip shrugged. "I guess she called yesterday crying. She said she wasn't going to come home."

I felt a moment of sympathy for James and, in spite of myself, admiration for him continuing to care for Sherry.

"By the way, how are things with you and Juanita?"

"Good." His smile blossomed. "She's a real neat person. Spunky and a lot of fun.

She's really working on changing her life, you know." This was delivered with a plaintive tone, just in case, I presumed, he thought I would be reporting back to Oden, Juanita's caseworker. "She hasn't been drinking or anything like that."

"That's good."

"I know she's not exactly the kind of person Mom, or even you, would pick out for me, but I do care for her. A lot."

Chip's perception was a welcome surprise. "Just like you guys have certain people in mind for me, I guess I've done the same for you. So if you care for her, then I'm glad. I hope Steve Stinson doesn't make trouble for you."

"I heard he's out of the county." Chip took a piece of raw onion and popped it in his mouth. Gross. "You know, speaking of having people in mind... James is also a really nice guy."

Why did even the mention of his name give me that silly jolt? "I'm sure he is," I conceded, trying to banish the memory of that foolish kiss out of my mind.

"I mean, look at him, taking care of that little baby for his sister. Not many guys would do that."

I let the observation slide as I tipped the onions into the sizzling frying pan, stirring them around to sauté them.

"Whatcha making?" Chip sniffed appreciatively. "Smells great."

Now, that was one thing I did appreciate about my brothers. As long as the scent of onion or bacon frying wafted through the house, they assumed supper was going to be fantastic. "Plain ordinary old shepherd's pie," I said, dumping the hamburger into the pan.

"You can make plain ordinary taste extraordinary."

My surprise was almost as great as the warm feeling his compliment gave me. "Thanks, Chip, that's nice to hear."

He beamed. "James told me it was a good idea to give you a compliment once in awhile."

Trust something James initiated to make me feel contradictory feelings of pleasure and frustration.

"So, would you be able to help James out?" Chip asked, as if his compliment had paved the way for my agreement. He leaned closer and smiled. "James told me to leave you alone. Said you worked hard enough every day, but I know that you're a good person and it would be great for him to get out."

"You're really on a roll," I said, shaking my head at his persistence and, secretly pleased with what James had told him. "Okay. I'll babysit Sherry."

"You're the best." Chip gave me an awkward one-armed hug. Then he clattered out of the kitchen, presumably to tell James the good news.

Nine o'clock. I wasn't going to get rescued from this screaming child for at least another hour. I had rocked, burped, fed, changed, sang, pulled faces, ignored and carried. Nothing in my babysitting repertoire had prepared me for this unceasing onslaught of grief.

Sherry's sorrow had worked up such a sweat on her, I had changed her clothes twice. My head ached and I wished for the tenth time I hadn't agreed to this.

"I'm a pretty easy touch," I said to Sherry. Not that she could hear me above her wails. I looked at the clock again. Seventeen seconds had passed.

I couldn't keep this up any longer, but what could I do?

WWMD. What would Mom do?

Though I could see the house from the window, I phoned my dad, hoping he would feel sorry for me and possibly spot me.

"Take her for a car ride," was his blunt advice.

I hung up and sighed. "Thanks, Dad," I said, and continued pacing. Five minutes later, I thought, why not?

So, ignoring her screams, I bundled Sherry up, carried her out to my car, which still had the baby seat in the front, and put the screaming bundle of baby girl in it, fighting her swinging arms to buckle her in.

I closed the door and fought the temptation to simply walk away. For a moment I understood what Laurel had to deal with and promised to be more sympathetic to her next time she called me at eleven o'clock at night.

A few minutes later I was driving down the road and, to my immense pleasure and surprise, Sherry's cries were slowly dissipating. Three miles down the road I could see her eyelids drooping, open, then droop again.

Then, thank the Lord, she was asleep. And, thank the Lord, I had a full tank of gas.

Though with the price of gas, this was turning into an expensive favor.

On a whim I turned down a side road and found myself heading toward the arena where the boys were working. I pulled up to the arena. So why did the sight of James's truck give my heart that little schoolgirl lift?

You should tell him that you're not going to babysit anymore. I glanced at Sherry. Easier said than done. No one had twisted my arm to take care of her. Well, James had put his hand on my shoulder and given me that too familiar half smile that started a small yearning deep inside.

The door of the arena opened and I was about to leave when Jace came out. He saw me, paused, then jogged over. I rolled down the window, pointed at Sherry and lifted my finger to my lips.

"What's up, sis? Should I get James?" he whispered, crouching down to my level.

"No. She wouldn't settle so I started driving with her and ended up here."

"Go inside. I'll drive her around for a bit if you want."

"No. That's okay."

"Really. You should watch James. He's really good."

"Now why would I want to watch him get tossed off a horse?"

"He's done the bronc riding. Alameda needed us to get the buck out of a couple of his geldings. James is doing the finesse work."

I had to admit I was curious. Jace sensed my hesitation, unbuckled my seat belt and pulled me out of the car. "I'll take care of the kid."

By that time I was out of the car and Jace was folding his six-foot-three frame into it, so there was nothing left to do but go inside. I pulled my coat close around me, wishing I had dressed a bit warmer, then walked over to the arena. The familiar smell brought back a flood of memories.

I climbed up a few dusty steps and dropped onto a rough wooden board that served as a seat.

Below me, the boys had set up a temporary round pen, and James was inside. His brown shirt had dust streaks on it from, I presumed, getting bucked off. His blue jeans were the same. He was throwing a rope at a horse, making him go round and round the metal pen. I knew roughly what he was doing. My brothers had tried their hand at "horse whispering" from time to time, but mostly they ended up "horse yelling."

Patience was not in their makeup.

But it seemed it was in James's. As I watched he kept the horse going, then, when the gelding was licking his lips, signaling his intention to "talk," James let him stop. He moved slowly toward the young horse, ran his gloved hands over his withers and down to his feet.

The horse shied away, and Chip and Neil groaned. But James only smiled and with a snap of his rope got him going in circles again.

Then James turned, looked up and saw me. He threw the rope at Chip. "Just get him doing what you want," he said. "Make it easy for him to do what you want, hard for him to do what he wants."

James vaulted over the boards and at my side, his cowboy hat still planted firmly on his head. "Sherry okay?" He pulled his gloves off and slipped them in the back pocket of his blue jeans. Dust streaked his face and he wiped his cheek with the back of his hand.

"She wouldn't quiet down, so I put her in the car and took her for a drive. Jace is with her now."

"I should go then." He was about to turn away, when I caught his arm and stopped him.

"No. She's fine for now. She'll settle once I get her back home." I let go of him, suddenly self-conscious and not particularly caring for the feeling. "Jace told me what you were doing and I, uh, wanted to see you work."

His smile was white against his dusty skin. "That's neat."

"Well, it's interesting. You do this often?" I glanced past him at Chip, who was trying, without much success, to emulate the smooth throws that James had been doing.

"Sometimes. Didn't always have time on the rigs. When my dad was still alive, he taught me what he knew." James rocked back on his heels, his hands in his back pockets, his eyes on me.

"So the whole bucking bronc thing…"

"Part of the training sometimes. But, I have to confess, I like to pit my skills against a bronc. From time to time. Very guy of me, I know."

I gave him a smile, pleased to see him still looking at me. "Well, you can't work against your nature, can you?"

"No. But like any good horse, a man can be trained. The trick is to make it hard to do the thing he wants to do and easy to do the thing he doesn't."

"Are you giving me an inside edge into the convoluted workings of a guy's mind?" I asked him with a laugh.

"Convoluted would be describing a woman's mind." This was said with another grin and a faint wink. Now normally winks don't do anything for me except set my teeth on edge, but somehow, from James, it seemed kind of cute. "Guys are straightforward. Eat. Work. Television. Sleep. Get up and do it again."

"Thanks for the invaluable lesson," I said. "I better get back to Sherry."

James glanced over his shoulder and pushed his cowboy hat back on his head and sighed. "Actually, I better take over. I shouldn't have asked you to do that for me. She's my responsibility." He looked back at me, his hazel eyes serious now. "Sorry about that. Chip said you really wanted to do that. I should have known better."

"Hey, don't blame yourself. Chip can be persuasive in his own way. And I didn't mind."

"You shouldn't lie." James angled me a knowing look. "You're not that good at it."

"Should I feel insulted?"

James laughed. "I think it was supposed to be a convoluted compliment. Sometimes guys can be complex." He pulled his hat off and ran his hands through his hair. Still shaggy. Still in need of a cut. Still looking good. He dropped his hat back on his head and blew his breath out through pursed lips. "Thanks for doing this, but I'll take her home."

"She's sleeping now. All I have to do is put her in bed."

"Then I'll follow you." He called out to my brothers, telling them that he was leaving with me. Chip nodded, then, when he thought I wasn't looking, high-fived his brother.

The drive home was quiet. Sherry still slept. The lights of James's truck hung behind me in my rearview mirror, high up. Though I like to think of myself as an independent woman—hear me roar when I find laundry on the floor—I found it comforting to know that this big truck with this big man was behind me. Keeping an eye on me.

"So, you're heading to the good life." Casey posed in the doorway of my office, holding a file folder in one hand, a briefcase in the other.

He was wearing his navy suit today and navy tie. The poster boy for government worker on his way to an important budget meeting. "I got a call from someone named Dan Crittenden asking for a reference." He nodded, his "knowing" look planted firmly on his face. "Nice fancy job for a nice fancy company. Guess you won't be getting your hands dirty working in the trenches."

I ignored the latter comment and pounced on the word "reference." "What did he want to know?" I asked, keeping my voice neutral and non-threatening. Casey had an interior geiger counter that could pick up eagerness vibes faster than you could say "balanced budget." Casey knew I wanted to leave, but if he knew how badly I wanted this job, I was sure he would find a way to mess it up. Casey was a happiness vacuum.

"I believe that would be classified information," he said with a curt nod of his head as he walked into my office.

I let him have his little secret.

"However, you are still an employee of the government and until you no longer are, I expect that the taxpayers shall continue to get full value for their dollar." His beady eyes bounced over my desk with its horizontal filing system. "And where shall I put this so you don't lose it?" He held out the file folder he had been carrying.

"What is it?" I cleared a space and took the file from him, refusing to apologize for the mess. My little rebellion.

"A new case for you. Henry had it but he has been less than diligent. I thought you could take care of it."

Usually I counted to twelve. Ten never gave me enough time to calm down, but I was latching on to the idea that I would be leaving so this time I only gave Casey seven. "I don't know if I want to be cleaning up after Henry. Why don't you give it to Oden?"

"Oden has a full case load."

And I didn't? I sighed, then flipped the file open and skimmed the particulars as best as I could.

A family of four. Absent mother. Father with alcohol problems. His name was Stan Bowick. Needed in-home support that Henry was supposed to arrange and hadn't. Sticky notes and papers that looked like they had been ripped out of old scribblers filled the file. "This is a boar's nest, Casey," I said, glancing up at him. "How am I supposed to make heads or tails of this?"

"You'll have to figure that out." He gave me what he thought of as a reassuring smile, then flicked the cuff of his white shirt and pointedly glanced at his watch. "Talk to Henry if you have any concerns." And off he pranced like he was the only busy person in this office and the rest of us peons spent most of our time sending jokes by e-mail.

I rubbed my forehead with my knuckles, grimacing at the ever-increasing workload. Sisyphus pushing the boulder up the hill had it easy compared to me. There was no way I was going to get all my paperwork done today. Or even tomorrow. I could sense panic creeping around the edges of the day, but I didn't dare indulge. I would get this done. It was just a matter of focusing. Staying on track. *Help me get this done, Lord,* I prayed. *These people are depending on me.*

I buzzed Bobby and told her to hold all my calls unless it was an emergency. I let her decide what constituted an emergency.

Ten minutes later, Bobby buzzed me back. "Sorry to bother you, but it's Laurel. She claims it's very serious."

As I picked up the phone, I sent up a prayer for patience.

"Hubie feels hot." Laurel was crying. "I don't know what to do."

No time. No time. The words resonated through my head as I cast a now panicked look over the files on my desk. "Did you take his temperature?"

"No." She sniffed. "His face is all red. I saw a program on TV? About kids that couldn't learn so good? This kid had the same thing?"

Deliver me from television diagnoses. "Laurel, take his temperature and if it's higher than normal, give him some Children's Tylenol. If that doesn't help bring it down, then take him to the hospital."

"But how do I know what normal is? I'm not a nurse."

I explained how to read a thermometer, trying to keep my own terror in check at my increasing workload. Then I hung up and promptly picked up the phone again to arrange some kind of help for the man with four kids. As I talked, I typed up a report for a court appearance I had to do next week.

An hour later Bobby put through an urgent

call from a lawyer representing the drunk mother of the two children I had apprehended last week. I disliked him from "hello" and liked him even less by "goodbye." Where was that good feeling I had about my work when I was sitting in church on Sunday? That whole idea of justice and mercy.

My tired mind stopped there a moment, remembering the sermon and how serious James looked when the minister was preaching. The sound of James's voice. How he looked at me and his nice smile. And his nice hair.

The shrill ring of the phone split through the moment. I pulled myself back to the present and the job that I was going to be leaving. Soon. Soon. The words were a soothing comfort.

It was seven o'clock before I finally dragged myself out of the office, angry with Casey, Henry, the pompous lawyer and Jace, who had called me to tell me that he and Dad were going to be late for supper, could I keep it warm for them?

Why did my brothers seem to think that my work was easier and less busy than theirs?

Maybe it's because they don't know?

The thought slid in behind my anger as I

walked across the still hot asphalt of the parking lot. I remembered James's words of a few days ago. Was he right? Did I simply let things happen and then react?

My car was still an oven by the time I got in, the heat of the day nicely trapped inside. I worked up a sweat starting it up. Of course the air conditioning wasn't working.

So down went the only window that worked, the passenger one, and of course the grader had been down our gravel road. Dust roiled up behind my car, into my car, into my mouth and hair.

On a scale of world suffering I knew my current irritations were minimal. I knew I had clients who were worse off than me. However I still felt cranky, out of sorts and sorry for myself by the time I pulled into our driveway. I needed to vent. Jace and Dad were going to be late and it looked like Neil and Chip weren't home yet.

Ten minutes later after changing into blue jeans and a shirt I was slipping a bridle over Spook's head and mounting up. It had been too long since I'd been on his back and I needed to get out, be on my own. Away from demands and people and expectations.

Spook danced around as I gathered up the reins. He didn't need much urging and soon he was trotting down a well worn path toward the open fields, the warm wind blowing all the cobwebs and dust out of my brain. Spook shook his head, impatient with this slow trot, but I held him in. I liked to keep things tame.

I got Spook down to a walk, but I could tell by the way he tossed his head and kept pulling on the reins he wasn't happy. I didn't care. For now I was content to follow the trail through the trees and simply enjoy the muffled sound of Spook's hooves on the ground, the mocking squawk of the magpies in the trees above. Half an hour later, duty tugged with relentless fingers, so I reluctantly turned Spook around to head back home. He shook his head and tried to go back the other way, but I was firm with him and he obeyed. We broke out into the open field and he started acting up again. After spending too much time cooped up in the smaller pasture he wanted to run.

Now I wasn't a galloper. I wasn't the kind of girl who imagined herself flying across field and dale, her hair streaming out behind her. One fact being that no matter how I shampooed, conditioned and treated, my hair would just flop. The other was that I was always a bit afraid when I galloped. When I was out with the boys, I let my horse run simply because if I didn't, I would be fighting my horse all the way home.

But after half an hour of holding Spook back, I was tired. Jace hadn't worked the fields yet, so I turned Spook around, clucked lightly and gave him his head. Spook bunched up his muscles, gave a couple of small hops and took off. I leaned forward, excitement threaded with fear, pounding through me. My hat blew off and my hair flapped behind me. Just like I figured it would.

But I wasn't going to get judged on artistic impression. And to my own surprise, in spite of my fear I was having fun. My fear melted away as exhilaration took over. Spook wouldn't let me fall, wouldn't go out of control. He wanted to run and I wanted to let him.

Spook's muscles were rippling under me, his head stretched out and I was completely focused on keeping my balance and not letting my feet slip out of the stirrups. On and on we ran, dirt flying up in great clods behind us.

Then we were bearing down on the

barnyard. I gently pulled him up. He shook his head, but obeyed and by the time we got close to James's house, which was beside the corral, I had Spook down to a quick trot. His best gait. I sucked in a deep breath, my face flushed and feeling as if I had adequately blown all the worries out of my brain.

The windows of James's house were open. And as I walked Spook past the house I heard it again. Sherry's keening wail.

Did that kid never settle?

In spite of the dust in my hair and the grit on my face, I could spare a moment of pity for James as I brought Spook into the corrals. James wasn't getting much work done on setting up that knitting shop, and I understood Robin hadn't called him yet.

By the time I had Spook's tack put away and had fed him some oats, I noticed that Jace, Chip and Neil were back. I needed to get going.

As I walked back toward the house, I stretched my arms over my head. Come morning, I was going to discover muscles I hadn't known of for a while.

Then, as I passed James's house, I caught the scent of supper cooking. I lifted my face, sniffed again, turning my head to catch the scent like a hound on a trail. Though I knew God could move mountains, I figured that getting the boys to cook was a larger task. So I could only conclude that the wonderful smells I was catching stomach-groaning whiffs of was coming from James's house.

At least he wasn't coming over to our house for supper.

I imagined my brothers sitting in the living room, waiting patiently, or impatiently, for their sister to serve them. I decided it wouldn't hurt them to wait a little longer. Besides, James probably needed some help with that baby and the neighborly thing to do was find out.

He was juggling Sherry, a phone tucked against his shoulder, and talking loudly over her wails. He held a bottle in his free hand and every now and then he jabbed it in the general direction of Sherry's mouth. She fought, bucked and pushed it away.

"Can I help?" I called out over the noise of Sherry's crying.

James whirled around and the look of relief on his face as I approached him with my arms out was the best sight I'd seen all day.

"I'll go wash my hands," I said and quickly cleaned up. Though my better judgment warned me against it, I allowed myself a glance at my reflection. Great. I cleaned my face as best as I could, but the strawlike tangle that was my hair, would have to wait until I showered. For now, I whisked my fingers through it and shrugged. From the sounds of Sherry's cries, James wasn't going to turn down my help based on the fact that I looked like a flushed scarecrow.

There was an awkward moment as I eased Sherry out of his arms. We bumped against each other, pulled away and finally I had the little babe cuddled against me, a bottle in her mouth while she sucked greedily at it.

James gave me a wink, then turned back to his phone conversation.

"What will the rent be for only half the building?"

I didn't mean to listen in, but the house was small and we were both in the living room and James was using the old-school phone that still hung on the wall. So he was tethered to the phone and I was kind of comfy curled up on James's leather couch with little Sherry. To keep my mind off James's conversation I talked to her.

"You're being a bad girl for your Uncle

James, you know," I said quietly, stroking her chubby hand with my pinky. Her fingers latched on while her plump lips worked the nipple, bubbles meowing their way up through the milk in the bottle. Large, round blue eyes stared up at me as if trying to decipher what I was doing in Uncle James's house.

"So if I can find another tenant, I can lease the whole complex for almost the same amount as what you were going to charge me for half," James barked.

I jumped, Sherry flinched and I quickly turned my attention back to her, soothing her with nonsense words. I would have sung, but I didn't want to create a psychosis in the poor child.

James paced the room as he negotiated and talked, then finally hung up. He stood with his back to me, his hands clasped behind his head, his hair sticking out from between his fingers.

"It's times like these that I understand the Old Testament prophets much better," James muttered.

"Pardon me?"

"You know, all those imprecations about fire and brimstone and pestilence. Don't you wish you could do some smiting sometimes?"

I thought about Casey and tried to imagine him with boils. "I'm more of a virtual reality smiter," I said. "In real life I would end up feeling sorry for the very people I was cursing."

He walked over and crouched beside me, his long fingers slipping through Sherry's curls. "That's because you've got such a soft heart."

"And because I'm such a soft touch. All people would have to do is make me feel guilty about what I've done and poof—" I waved my hand "—gone would be the sores and the palsy and the Hittites and Jebusites."

"You're more of a New Testament person than I am," he said quietly. "I think us guys prefer all those kings waging battle on other kings and eye-for-eye stuff. A little easier to work with than loving your enemy and doing good to those that hurt you."

"I don't think women have an easier time with that," I said quietly, watching how his hand so gently cradled his niece's head. "I think we have fewer options. Getting physical against an enemy isn't as easy as it is for men."

He smiled up at me. "I learn something from you every day."

I looked down at him, remembering the kiss we shared the last time I held his little niece. That kiss had been a mistake, I knew that. But for a brief moment, I wanted to repeat it. Try it one more time to see if that spark I had felt was real, or simply the imaginings of a lonely woman.

He rides broncs. Plays hockey.

Goes to church, takes care of his niece. Makes supper, from the smells I caught coming from the kitchen.

He's a guy. He is staying in Preston and he's going to settle here. You'll never get away from your brothers or from Casey or from the relentlessness of your job.

I thought of Les. He was interested, he lived in the city and wore a suit and went to plays and offered to help me find an apartment when I moved. Which, from the way Casey was talking, was a fairly sure thing.

"Did you have a nice ride?"

My face flushed as I realized he must have seen my madcap race back home. "Yeah. I needed to get rid of some frustration."

He tilted his head to one side, studying me. "Pushing limits can accomplish that."

"That's why you like to ride broncs?"

"Yeah, but if I really want to live on the edge, I go grocery shopping without a list."

"You're a madman."

James chuckled and then a sharp rap on the door brought him to his feet.

"Is Danielle here?" Neil stuck his head in the door, caught sight of me and stepped inside. "Great. There you are. We were wondering when supper is. Chip has to head out to Kolvik to charm his little honey."

I glanced down at Sherry. She was almost finished her bottle. "I'll be there once this little munchkin is done."

"Oh, don't worry about that, sis. James can feed her."

He sounded so reasonable I almost thought he was giving me a chance to get away, when in fact he was saying he needed me. Now. I glanced up at James, who shook his head, as if telling me to be firm.

But now I was cornered. If I left now I would feel manipulated by my brothers. If I stayed, by James.

"Can I ask a favor of you?" James caught my indecision. "I need to make a bunch of phone calls. If you take Sherry to your place, I'll bring over the supper I've got cooking in the oven and share it with you and your family."

Neil sniffed then nodded. "Smells like lasagna. You got enough?"

"Plenty. Is that okay with you?" James asked, turning to me.

"Sounds like a plan for me," I said, trying not to be embarrassed by Neil's forthrightness and, at the same time, thankful for James's diplomacy.

I pulled the bottle out of Sherry's mouth, surprised at how strong her sucking reflex was. She batted at the bottle then started wailing when she realized nothing more was coming.

James had the phone in his hand, ready to make another call. There was no way he could carry on a conversation with this blessed infant carrying on, so I left.

The phone was jangling when I got into the house. Ignoring it wasn't in my genetics so I let Sherry's diaper bag slip off one arm as I juggled her to other. I caught the phone on the fourth ring.

"Hey, hon. I'm at loose ends next week," Mrs. Woytowich was saying in a relentlessly cheerful voice. "Can I come and clean your house for you?"

Was this woman for real? Asking if she could clean my house? "Of course...I mean, that would be wonderful. Please and thank you and all kinds of other gratitude…" I couldn't spill the words fast enough. "That would be wonderful."

"Does nine o'clock on Tuesday work out for you?"

Midnight, early morning, anything would work out for me, I thought as my eyes swept over the room. Clothes in various states of cleanliness lay scattered over the furniture, plates from breakfast and lunch were spread out on the counter. Would simply piling them on top of one another threaten my brother's manliness?

"That would be perfect." I glanced at the calendar and my heart fell. "Actually, Dad has an appointment with his doctor that day…." I let the sentence hang, wondering what she would do with the information.

"Oh, don't worry about that. I can bring him. That way you don't have to take time off work and deal with that little snake, Casey."

Snake. Casey. I felt an un-Christian shot of relief that I wasn't the only person who knew what Casey was and thought the same of him. "How do you know my boss?"

"I've had dealings with him in the past,"

Mrs. W. said. "He's pompous and self-righteous. I wish someone would tell him off."

I did, too. But I wasn't going to take any chances on being the one. He could be vindictive and nasty when crossed and until I was packing up my desk to leave, I was stuck with putting up with him.

The thought sent a searing shot of torment through my stomach. *Please, Lord,* I prayed, *let me get that job.*

"Anyhow, you don't worry about your father or your house. I'll come and take care of things."

She asked a few more questions about the house, told me what she needed to have ready when she came. She wanted a list. A list! I couldn't believe the blessing that had been dropped in my lap. *Thank You, Lord.*

I said goodbye, hung up the phone and grinned down at Sherry, who had settled down nicely. "Did you hear that? Mrs. Woytowich wants me to make her a list? A list." I repeated the words again, making them real. "And your Uncle James is bringing supper, which means I don't have to cook for those hulking brothers of mine who don't know the meaning of the words 'move out.'" I sank into my dad's recliner, ignoring the blue jeans draped over the arm. I pulled up the footrest, appreciating the luxury of a few moments of empty time.

Sherry finally lay quiet in my arms, warm, soft and sweet-smelling. I stroked her petal soft cheek, relishing this gentle moment. She gurgled, tiny spit bubbles forming at the corners of her Cupid-bow lips as she waved her arms and kicked her feet with jerky little baby movements.

"Now that you're not crying, you are adorable," I cooed, stroking her cheek with my finger. She smiled, her little teeth glinting at me. "And I'm busy right now, taking care of you so I can't set the table. My lazy brothers are going to have to do that."

Sherry cooed, then clapped her hands as if celebrating with me. A vague thought circled the edges of my mind, slowly taking shape. *I wonder what it would be like to have a child of my own.*

I touched Sherry's cheek again, let my hand linger then caught myself mid-mush. I had plans. I had a future. It was in the city doing a job that didn't require dealing with the roughest elements of society.

*But would you enjoy it? Wouldn't you miss
the challenge?*

Stay focused, I reminded myself. Stay
with the plan.

Chapter Ten

I kept my eyes on my plate and struggled to finish the small piece of lasagna I had taken. I took a quick drink of water, which helped get the dry, overcooked piece of pasta down. Another drink diluted the over-salted sauce. Around me my brothers were wolfing down a second helping.

"That was great, James." My dad wiped his mouth, threw his napkin on his plate and sat back, patting his stomach.

"Yeah. You'll make some lucky woman a great husband," Chip agreed, scraping the last of the lasagna off his plate.

I had set my culinary bar too high, I thought as I worked down the last mouthful of leathery lasagna. All these years of sautéing and fussing and seasoning were obviously wasted on my brothers. I could have saved myself a lot of work if their effusive compliments were anything to go by.

"Good food, eh, Danielle?" Jace subtly nudged me with his elbow.

"Great." Sherry squawked and I jumped up. "Oh goodness, I better get her changed."

"Didn't you do that before supper?" James asked.

"Yeah, but I think she needs another one." I gave him an apologetic smile, excused myself and got up. Once in the bathroom I quickly spit out the last bit of food I had squirreled away in one cheek and rinsed out my mouth. Sherry's diaper was dry, as I knew it would be. I needed the excuse to get rid of the last of my supper.

I set Sherry on the floor and as I quickly washed my hands I glanced at myself in the mirror. Flushed cheeks, bright eyes. Wasn't caused by the food, that was for sure. The company?

Try as I might, I couldn't eradicate James's kiss or the moments that led up to it. He could actually be serious. Talk about going to church. Then he actually came to church.

He was messing with my plans and my mind.

He's attractive and pleasant and you like him.

He's a lousy cook. Aren't men supposed to be good cooks? They are in all the movies.

At least he tried. When was the last time any of your brothers did more than open a can of readymade soup? Admit it, you like him.

Sherry kicked her feet, as if trying to get my attention and her little running shoe fell off. I bent over to pick it up and then someone was knocking on the door.

"Everything okay in here?"

James.

Heat chased up my cheeks, making them even pinker than they were. "I'll be right there," I said, quickly wetting a face cloth with cold water and pressing it against my face. For good measure I switched the water to warm and quickly wiped Sherry's shining cheeks. She twisted her head away and started to cry. I picked her up, cuddled her close and then opened the door.

James stood in the doorway, his arm resting against it. He smiled as I came out and held out his hands for his niece. "I'll take her."

"I don't mind." And I didn't. Sherry was a

cute little bundle when she wasn't howling, and I didn't often have the chance to cuddle a happy baby.

The boys and Dad were already in the living room arguing about which sports program they were going to watch. Dad was in remarkably high spirits.

The dishes scattered over the table, not so good. Guess I would have to postpone the baby cuddling for a while. I was about to hand Sherry to James when I stopped, looked from the kitchen to my brothers to James, who was watching me to see what I would do.

I may be slow, but I can be taught. Eventually. If I didn't start training these guys now, they would be at a loss by the time I left.

"Hey, guys, how about some help with the dishes?" Okay, not exactly firm and forceful, but hopefully they got the message.

Neil looked at me. Frowned. "What did you say?" Had I just spoken in some foreign language? I guess I should be glad he noticed me. Chip and Jace were still flipping through the channels, intent on maximizing their sports absorption. Obviously a firmer direction was needed.

I walked to the living room, still holding

Sherry. "Neil, you can clear the table and take care of the leftovers. Chip and Jace, you guys can wash and dry." I looked at my dad sitting comfortably in his recliner and realized that he needed to participate, as well. "Dad, you know where everything goes, you can put the dishes away."

Four pairs of eyes stared at me, as if I had suddenly mutated into a puzzling subspecies of sister and daughter. I found their lack of jumping-to-it disturbing. "Now," I said, as if talking to a group of school children.

Then, like a dream, four figures lumbered to their feet and slowly moved past me to the kitchen, tatters of sighs drifting back as they passed.

James gave me a thumbs-up sign behind their backs.

"You have to help, too, dude," Chip called out to James.

"Nope. I'm exempt. I made supper."

Chip shrugged. "Fair enough." And that was that.

I stayed a moment, watching the unreal scenario of my brothers and father working in the kitchen. Water sloshed on the floor, knives fell and the banter rose to a dull roar as towels snapped and plates crashed into the dishwasher.

I had to get out of here.

Sherry and I settled on one corner of the couch and to my surprise and discomfort, James settled in on the other, his long legs spread out in front of him.

"Feels good doesn't it?" He slid me a smile. "Being all bossy and in charge."

"A wonderful sense of power," I admitted. "My brothers are an occasional mystery, but sometimes they do surprise me."

"Like I said, they like you. They just need some guidance." He turned serious. "They're also lucky to have you."

His unexpected compliment brought a flush to my cheeks.

"Really. Robin has been…" He let the sentence drift off as he shook his head. "All her life I've been there for her, then she disappears for a year and shows up with a baby that she casually dumps on me and leaves." He dragged his hand over his face and blew out a sigh. "What am I supposed to do with her?"

I was at a loss, as well, but abandoned and neglected children were part of my job. For now. "If you want I could look at in-home care for Sherry or, failing that, place her in a temporary foster home." I looked down at Sherry, who lay, for now, contentedly in my arms. Her mouth was pursed up, her lips moving up and down as if she were getting the dregs out of a phantom bottle.

"No way."

The strength of his tone made me look up. James eyes snapped to mine, blazing with an intensity that took my breath away. "I'd never let anyone else take care of my niece. She's my responsibility and I care about her."

I nodded slowly and held up a hand in a reconciling gesture. "I'm getting that," I said quietly, pleased at his defense of this little girl. In my line of work I saw so few guys take responsibility for their own children, that it was heartwarming to see this man so defensive of a niece.

"Sorry about the high drama moment," he said, settling back with an embarrassed look. "Robin and I have only ever had each other. I've always been the one to take care of her."

"So you've been enabling a sibling, as well," I said, with a knowing lift of my eyebrows.

James threw me a puzzled glance, then one corner of his mouth lifted in a half smile.

"I've only been enabling one, you've been working on three and a father."

"I qualify for a group rate." I shrugged. "Robin's lucky to have you looking out for her." The vaguely winsome note slipped unexpectedly into my voice. For a moment I was jealous of Robin.

"In their own convoluted way your brothers look out for you, too."

I heard the crash of some plates and Neil's voice chastising Chip, telling him to be careful. "You think?" I asked, grimacing.

"I know. They talk about you lots and not just in a housekeeper or cook capacity."

My brothers weren't given to random acts of affection and their body language was unreadable. But James's comment gave me a sliver of hope for appreciation when I was gone. That and the sounds of progress being made coming out of the kitchen.

"So what are you going to do about Robin?" I asked, cuddling Sherry a little closer. She yawned, batted her hand in the air, then slowly let it drop as her eyes slid shut.

"Besides hunting her down and reading her the riot act?" He scratched his chin with his forefinger, then shrugged. "Not much I can except wait for her to start feeling maternal. The biggest problem with that plan of inaction is that in the meantime I'm trying to set up this business and toting a baby is really putting a crimp in my style."

"Now seriously, what kind of business are you setting up?" I asked. "I have this inkling it's not a knitting shop." I shifted the now sleeping Sherry in my arms, getting a bit more comfortable.

"How do you know?" He canted his head to one side, granting me a semiflirtatious sidelong glance.

It made me feel a little wobbly. "I know, because you don't have knitter's shoulder," I joked, hoping to allay the sensations his attention gave me.

A slow smile slipped across his face. "Okay. I'll bite. What is knitter's shoulder?"

I looked away, the wobbly sensation increasing. "A condition that affects chronic knitters," I said, trying to sound serious. "After prolonged periods of knitting the right shoulder twitches upward at one-second intervals."

"You're making that up."

I sighed my defeat. "I thought I was better than that."

He laughed lightly. "I don't think you know how to lie."

"Oh, don't grant me sainthood yet," I said. "In grade four I told Tommy Petrenko that I knew how to drive a tractor when it was really Jace who was driving. He just let me steer."

"How old was Jace?"

"Probably about fourteen." I had forgotten how Jace used to let me "help" him drive when he was baling straw in the fall. Everyone had a job during harvest. Chip would be with Mom, who drove the grain truck between the fields and the yard, Neil would be back at the farm to help with unloading and Dad would be combining. Jace would take me in the tractor while he baled straw. My job was to make sure the baler wasn't plugging up and to count bales. My best days were the ones when Jace let me "drive" the tractor even though he was barely old enough to be driving himself.

"That's a wonderful memory," James said quietly.

"Yeah. It is." I smiled thinking about it. Even got a momentary warm feeling about my brothers, which was kind of unusual these days. I turned back to James, feeling all mellow. "So, really, what are you figuring on doing?"

"Actually I've been dabbling in restoring older cars. I've been getting busier with it and thought I would give a shot at doing it full-time."

"Hence the lease on the building."

"Hence." He laughed. "I didn't think people used that word anymore."

"It's in the social worker phrase book. 'At age six, Zeke was pushed out of the line for the slide at the playground, *hence* his use of his fists to make his point with the current caseworker.'"

"You ever get hit?"

"By some of the younger clients. I've been threatened by the older ones."

"You sound so casual about it. Aren't you ever afraid?"

"Sometimes. I pray a lot and trust that God will protect me." I thought of Steve Stinson. He was one person who genuinely gave me the creeps, but so far I haven't had to deal with him again. I hoped Chip wouldn't, either.

"So you have your extreme moments in your line of work, as well."

"I suppose I do, though I don't think of it that way. It's part of my job."

Another shared smile. This time I didn't look away, though I should have. James's expression grew serious and our previous kiss loomed large between us. I had to forget it. I had to keep my eye on the prize. A shiny new job in the city.

So why didn't I break the connection? It was simple kinetics. Lower chin, move eyes. Invisible hands held my head, kept me looking at him. Losing my breath.

"So, dishes are done, wicked stepsister. Anything else on your agenda?" Neil called out as he, Chip and Jace trooped into the living room.

My heart started up again, thudding in my chest. I diverted my attention to my brothers.

"Where's Dad?" I asked.

"He's still trying to figure out where to put the salad spoons." Jace dropped into one of the easy chairs and kicked aside the pile of newspapers on the coffee table so he could put his feet there. "We could have told him, but what would be the fun in that?"

Chip sat on the couch between us and Jace shot him a warning look. Oblivious to Jace's unspoken hint, Chip slouched down, wiggled a bit to get comfortable and folded his hands over his stomach. "Any word on that lease yet?" he asked James, rolling his head sideways.

James didn't say anything. Chip poked him. "Yo. James, my man. Talking at ya."

James blinked, as if coming from a ways away, then gave Chip an apologetic look. "Sorry, brain freeze."

"Asking about the lease."

James nodded and brought them up to date on his progress. "So I need a tenant for the other half of the building." He glanced from Neil to Chip. "You guys have been complaining long enough about your boss. What do you think of starting up your own place? Taking up the other half of the lease on the building I'm looking at. I'd cut you a deal."

"I tried that already," Chip sighed. "No joy with the bank people."

The despondent note in his voice brought out my maternal instincts. I wanted to put my arm around him and comfort him. In spite of his tattoos and tough talk, he was a softie and I didn't want to see him disappointed again.

"I know. Neil told me," James said. "But

if you had a backer, I'm sure you could get the money from the bank."

"And where would I get a backer?"

James leaned forward looking from Neil to Chip, his expression serious. "I've got a bunch of money set aside. I'd be willing to put up the money in your business as a silent partner."

I couldn't help but stare. James would put his own money on the line so Chip could realize a dream?

"That's quite a risk for you, son," my father put in as he came into the room. He must have found a final resting place for the salad spoons. He lowered his head toward Jace, who sighed and got up from my father's chair. "Are you sure you want to take it?" he asked as he settled in and folded his arms across his chest.

"I trust Chip and Neil. I think they would do well."

Neil's eyes lit up like a Christmas tree. Chip jumped to his feet and cheered, then turned to James. "You sure, dude? I mean, it's a lot of cash. You win a lottery or something?"

James shook his head. "No. My parents had an insurance policy and I spun my share into my contracting business. When I sold it, my money had made me more money. I want to settle down and get it working for me again. I figured helping you guys start up a mechanic's shop would be a start."

I couldn't help but feel a rush of gratitude as I saw the stunned looks on my brothers' faces. Owning their own shop was something they had dreamed of ever since they started working for Ernie Smith, a man who could give Casey a few lessons on how to be a miserable boss. Even more, the boys knew full well the difference between the shop rates and what they were getting paid, but in a town the size of Preston, other employment opportunities in their chosen field were hard to come by. Neither of them wanted to work in an oilfield.

Now, thanks to James, they had a chance to realize a faint dream.

Jace pulled out a pad of paper, my father provided a pen and on the now cleared coffee table of the living room, they drew up a rough business plan. The mood in the room was one of celebration.

So I kept my own news about my potential job to myself. It was no secret that I'd been looking, but the boys were of the opinion that if they pretended it wasn't going to happen, it wouldn't.

Soon, I decided. They needed to be prepared, but it might be better to wait until it was a done deal and I had a firm job offer in my hands.

Sherry shifted in my arms and I tried to get comfortable, but James noticed me fiddling around. He put his hands on his knees and shoved himself to his feet. "I'd love to sit and make more plans with you guys, but I should get my niece to bed."

I gave him a grateful look and carefully shifted to get up. Letting sleeping babies lie was a good maxim here.

James gave me his hand and I reluctantly took it, letting him pull me to my feet.

I wasn't going to look at the avid audience that was my brothers. I knew for them this little family moment was like icing on the cake for them. First the mechanic shop looked to be a reality and now their sister was holding hands with the man they tapped to be their future brother-in-law.

Don't count your chickens, I thought, pulling my hand a little too quickly out of James's.

James and I were quiet on the short walk

back to the house. I could have given Sherry to him, but I was reluctant to let go of her and, I reasoned to myself, I didn't want to jostle her unnecessarily.

Her arms flung out when I laid her in the crib, but then she snuffled, and her fingers relaxed, curling back against her palm. I covered her with a blanket and then quietly walked out of the room.

James stood in the living room, his back to me. He spun around and as I carefully closed the door, he came closer, coming to a stop bare inches away.

"Obviously she settled okay. I don't hear her crying," he said quietly.

"She's fine. I hope she sleeps the rest of the night for you." I glanced up at him, then away. I knew I should be going, but some unseen force had me rooted to the spot.

"By the way, thanks for supper," I said.

"You didn't eat much."

"Wasn't that hungry."

"Too much salt, right?"

"That and a few other things." I flashed him an apologetic smile. "I guess I should have said that more diplomatically."

"No. No. Honesty is good." He shifted his

weight, which brought him even closer to me. "I like that about you."

"Blame it on living with four guys who've never met a cellophane bag they can't poke a hole in to get what they need." I thought a joke might lighten the atmosphere, which was shifting toward potential relationship stuff. Like it had the other night.

But he didn't even smile. He didn't say anything. My cue to leave. The longer I stayed here the more my brothers would speculate. But my feet seemed to have developed some type of palsy and stayed where they were.

I lived in a crowded house, was busy all day with other people, I had good friends, a strong relationship with the Lord, but it was a gentle yearning for a relationship, a basic girl/guy loneliness I didn't want to analyze that kept me rooted to the spot.

James's face was a foot away from mine and when he lifted his arm and placed his hand on the frame of the door behind me, the foot became mere inches. I swallowed, but kept myself statue still. I wasn't going to make the first move. In fact I wasn't going to make any move. In a few weeks I was going to be away from Preston and living in the city and…

Then James lowered his head as his eyes drifted shut. I kept mine open to anchor myself in reality as his lips met mine. He pulled back a hair's breadth and his breath feathered over my cheek. I swallowed as my heart started up. Time wheeled slowly, slowly.

The practical part of me resisted. But the other, lonely, yearning, romantic part that was attracted to James, wouldn't.

Gradually, I closed the distance between us, let my hand drift up his chest, over his neck and tangle in his hair at the nape of his neck.

I knew I had to stop. So why couldn't I? Was I so shallow that all James had to do was come close and I was kissing him?

"What's happening here, Dani?" James whispered, his use of my nickname sending little flutters of intimacy chasing down my spine.

I swallowed as I slowly let my hand drift down his shoulder. I straightened his collar, smoothed down the front of his shirt, reluctant to let go of this fragile contact. "I don't know," I whispered.

He brushed his lips over the top of my head, lowered his hand to my face and cupped my chin, lifting my face to look at him.

"You're an amazing person, you know. I knew that from the first time I saw you." His voice was pitched low and soft, and his words wrapped me in warm comfort.

Until they penetrated to the analytical part of my brain. And I remembered how we first "met." I concentrated on the fold of his collar in an attempt to distract myself from his gentle smile and the glow of his eyes.

"I need to know something, James," I said, smoothing the collar down. "When you took me out the first time, you were talking about Schubert and poetry."

James nodded, moving in again. I put my hand on his warm chest, trying to ignore the steady thump of his heart. "Was that real or fake?"

James drew back, looking puzzled. "What do you mean?"

I was going to stay casual about it. Be a woman of the world. But the James of that "date," the James of the "Jigs" and the James that I was getting to know were getting inextricably intertwined. I didn't know which one was real and which one was put on.

"The whole bet thing you had going with my brothers when you were...Jigs. Your alter ego. The bet that you could fool me and take me out. When did that stop and…" I was about to add "and this begin," but I didn't want to put a voice to what we had just shared. It was so fragile and uncertain and I wasn't sure myself where to put it alongside the bet my brothers had made with him or where it fit with plans that were slowly coming to realization.

"What?" There was no way James could fake the frown that creased his brow and for a moment I wondered if I should carry on. But I had begun this and knew that I needed to finish it. The longer I spent with James, the more confused I became.

"I heard my brothers saying that they had made a bet with you. That you wouldn't be able to get me to go out with you. When you were…Jigs. Your alter ego."

James pulled away, scratching his cheek with his forefinger. "There was never any bet, Danielle."

Chapter Eleven

I stared at him. "What do you mean, no bet? There was a bet. I heard Neil and Chip say so."

James's frown grew hard and for a moment I wished I hadn't even brought it up. "What do you mean there *was* a bet?"

"The day I met you at the garage where they work I heard the guys say that they bet I would come around. Chip said he would take that."

James held his hand up as if to stop me. "They may have said bet and you may have heard it, but I never took them up on it. I treated it as a joke, but I wasn't part of it."

Part of me heard and acknowledged this, but the part that still hurt carried on. "What about showing up at the restaurant the next day. You had shaved and were wearing decent clothes. You were James and you were different...."

James gave me a feeble smile. "Not completely different."

"And what about the Schubert and the poetry? Was that part of it?"

He stepped back holding his hands up in a gesture of surrender. "Okay, that was laying it on a bit thick."

My heart fell. "So it *was* part of the bet."

"How many times do I have to tell you, there was no bet." James stood with his hands on his hips. "The day I saw you after I met you for the first time, I had a meeting with a guy about leasing this building and I saw you, and said hi and you were friendly, which was a real switch from the last time I saw you, and by the time I realized you didn't recognize me, well..." He lifted his shoulder in a negligent shrug. "I didn't think there was anything wrong in capitalizing on it."

I jumped on the last thing he said. "Capitalizing on it?"

"Well, yeah." He gave me his now patented crooked grin and took a step closer. "I could tell you liked me and I liked you." He shrugged. "I figured it was my chance."

"Chance?"

"For a social worker who uses the word 'hence' you sure seem to have lost your grip of the English language."

"So even though the set-up wasn't about a bet, you were still playing me. Laughing at me. Treating me like a joke. Not much different than a bet, I would say."

"The only joke is the way you're reacting to this." He gave me a crooked grin, which was, I guessed, supposed to make me smile. Instead it only increased my anger. "You should feel flattered that I cared enough to research some dead composer and pretend I knew what I was talking about," he continued.

"Flattered?" I glared at him. "That you wanted to deliberately fool me into thinking you were someone you weren't?"

"Not deliberately. I was utilizing an advantage. And from what your brothers told me about you, I needed every 'in' I could get."

"In? What do you mean, 'in'?"

"Your brothers told me that you were a hard sell. That you were tough and independent but that you liked poetry and music and other things like that. I have never met anyone like you before and from the moment

I saw your picture in the garage where your brothers worked, I knew I wanted to meet you. Then I saw you in the grocery store and then at Neil and Chip's garage and you brushed me off like a fly."

"I brushed you off because you had blood-shot eyes and wouldn't help me with the tire." I glared at him as something else registered. "Tough and independent?"

"I had welder's flash."

"What?"

"The bloodshot eyes. I got those from welding. And your own brothers told me you were tough. That's why I didn't do anything when you came into the shop with that flat tire and then, later, when that Stinson guy was threatening you."

"I wouldn't have minded some help then."

"Tough and independent, remember?"

"I'm not that tough. You make me sound like I should be spitting out nails, which I don't. Steve Stinson scares me and there you were spouting off about Schubert and poetry," I said, trying to sort through what I was hearing. "You've got some convoluted idea of what a woman wants," I said, my anger spilling out now.

"Actually, from the sounds of things I have no idea at all what a woman wants. Which, by the way, makes me *exactly* like most guys *and* men on this planet."

"Well, I should know because I live with four of them and work for one of them and it shouldn't surprise anyone why I want to leave."

By this time we were standing almost nose-to-nose, glaring at each other, angry words swirling around us like a noxious cloud.

How had we gone from tender kiss to Armageddon?

James held my eyes, his own narrowing. "You're still leaving?"

"The sooner I get out of here, the better." But somehow the words didn't have the conviction they once had.

Did I really still want to move away? I hadn't heard anything from Dan Crittenden or Les Steglund. They would call. I still had a plan. Something would come up. Eventually.

But James…

I shook my head to dispel the doubts, the questions. This shouldn't be happening now. Surely I wasn't such a ninny that a few kisses from someone that my brothers tried to set me up with and had pushed on me at every opportunity would make me change my entire plan for my life.

What you feel is a result of more than a few kisses.

Okay, I was really getting tired of this voice in my head. She had to go.

What do you mean? She is me! I'm just as much a part of this discussion as you are.

Was arguing with myself the first sign of ill mental health? Or was paying attention to the voice?

"Yes. I'm going." I repeated the words, trying to silence my "other" voice.

"To some fancy job in the city where men are men and wear suits and order grande non-fat lattes, no foam with room from a barista at some coffee bar who acts like knowing how to do this makes him all suave when really, it's still just coffee."

"And this is a bad thing?" I had to think of Les and the coffee we'd had together.

"No, but I don't think this is your thing."

"You know, this is exactly the attitude I've been fighting for years. My brothers and my father and my mother all seem to know exactly what I want, but somehow, they all miss the mark, as you just found out." I clenched my hands into fists, drawing out memories to shore my thoughts. "All my life everything was about the guys and guy stuff. Never once was what I wanted taken into consideration. We went to rodeos, hockey tournaments and tractor pulls. All because that was what the guys wanted. No one ever asked me what I wanted. Now I find out they assumed I was exactly like my mother, which I'm not. At all. I'm not tough. I cried every time I had to watch *Where the Red Fern Grows,* my dad's favorite movie, and I like to have a man take care of me even though my own job seems to put me in guy vicinity every day. And now, I want to move to the city and work at a civilized job. I want to be able to order a stupid cappuccino and not get a blank look. I want to go to plays and I want to finally, for the first time in my life, dress up in a velvet dress, put on full makeup and go to the *Nutcracker Suite* at Christmas instead of sitting in a chilly hockey arena cheering on a bunch of brawling brutes, who will end up at the bar celebrating their win or commiserating with each other over their loss."

James didn't laugh. He didn't even smile. All he did was touch my cheek ever so lightly, as if he understood. "You can still do that from here. Because no matter what you say I doubt that working in a highrise doing clean, tidy work that only benefits a select few will make you feel as fulfilled as your current job does."

I stared at him. "And what do you know about my current job?"

James moved his head closer, but I didn't budge. I was not going to be intimidated. "I know that you work too hard, that your boss is a jerk, that you should tell him where to get off and that I think it's easier for you to run away to the city than it is to face some of the things that you should be facing right here, right now."

"I face them every day. It's all about changing the things I can and that whole serenity prayer thing. I want a safe, stable and tame life."

"Do you really? When I saw you racing across the field on that horse of yours, I didn't see a safe, tame girl. I saw someone who enjoyed pushing boundaries. I think you like a wild and uncertain world. You just need to learn to control it instead of running away."

A memory slowly surfaced. My brothers

pushing me to get back on a horse that had just bucked me off. I was crying and afraid and angry with them, but we were miles from nowhere and the only way to get back was either to walk, or ride. So, with tears running down my cheeks, I got back on the horse. For the first mile I was trembling and jumped each time the horse did. Finally, I was so worn out and angry, I started making the horse trot. By the time we got home, I was angry with my brothers, but, at the same time, exhilarated that I had overcome this fear.

James touched my face, trying to draw out a confession. "I know that your job is challenging and hard and dirty and nasty and that if you didn't do it, then maybe someone else would, but most social workers like you, who really care about their clients, are a gift. I know that you have a gift from God to care about people and to help them and that you're good at your job."

I looked at him as his words washed over me in a wave of leashed anger and frustration, yet something lay deeper than his words. Some emotion that I hardly dared acknowledge, because that would mean backing out, proving my brothers right. Proving James right.

He pulled in a long slow breath, as if to slow himself down. "Now that we've traded soliloquies, I need to tell you that I don't think you'll be happier with that job, Dani. I think you'll miss the very things that make you frustrated with your work now. You'll miss the challenges. The need to do something that makes a difference. Much as you say you don't seek it, I think you'll miss living on the edge."

I looked at James, holding his gaze that was now intently fixed on me. "I won't miss my boss."

"Then change that." His hand moved up, tangling itself in my hair, anchoring my head to his hand. I wanted him to stop, but I didn't want to move away.

I didn't know what I wanted anymore, only that being here, so close to James, was like puzzle pieces clicking into place.

"I can't change him. I can't get rid of him. So how I can stay…not liking my boss…not liking where my life is now." I was stuttering, but I didn't know how to tell him how frightened his words were making me.

"You're not as powerless as you think, Dani. You can do something about your circumstances."

"Like what?" My former frustration returned, the same feeling of being locked into a place I wasn't happy or content, a place I could see no way around but escape. "Arrange for a mysterious accident? Besides breaking the Sixth Commandment, it's illegal."

James slipped his hand through my hair, loosening his grip on me for a moment. "Look at what happened with your brothers this evening. Did you ever think you would see the day that they did the dishes?"

"They didn't do it on their own," I protested, struggling to keep my mind focused while his finger moving gently over my neck threatened to distract me. His face, inches from mine, tangled my emotions until I didn't know exactly what I wanted anymore.

"Exactly," James said, his deep voice growing quieter. More intimate. "You told them what they needed to do. You pushed them. Guys need that whether we want to admit it or not. And thanks to you I'm finding my way back to the Lord."

I was growing bewildered and, to tell the truth, a bit scared. I had a plan. It was sound.

To abandon it now, to try something else, to stay here created a low-level panic in me. I had to think.

"I care about you, Danielle," he said quietly. "And I care that you're not happy right now. I've been there and I know what it feels like, but I've learned to make changes where I can and adjust where I can't."

"Right. And that's what I'm doing," I said, breathless now. "Adjusting where I can't. By getting another job."

"I don't think that's going to make a difference." James brushed his lips gently over my cheek again. "If you can't be happy here, I don't know if you can be happy there." He kissed me lightly then pulled back. "And I want you to be happy here. Very badly."

I closed my eyes, shutting out the sight of his handsome face shadowed by whiskers, his hazel eyes speckled with gold.

He was confusing me with his seductive voice, his gentle hand, his appealing presence. When he bent and kissed me again, I knew I couldn't stay here. Not like this.

It took more willpower than I thought I possessed, but I pushed myself away from the wall, away from James. "Thanks for the pep talk," I said, pasting a smile on my face. "I'll keep it in mind as I'm packing up."

Though I knew the expression, "his face fell" and had read it numerous times in books and articles, I didn't truly experience it until now. And in that slow drift of James's expression from encouragement to frustration, I had to fight the urge to recant my glib words. I couldn't explain to myself why I didn't want him disappointed in me. I knew I didn't like how he was looking at me now.

But I couldn't back out now. Though I didn't have the job yet, I felt as if my life was gaining momentum in the direction I had been pushing toward for many, many years. I had prayed about this and now Mrs. Woytowich was coming to clean my house and watch Dad. Things were coming into place. I couldn't stop this now. Not for some guy who was good-looking and fun and intelligent and a Christian…

I spun around and walked out of the house before I could be drawn away from my plan. My own plan. Not anyone else's.

The knock on the door sent my heart up into my chest.

I retied my hair into a ponytail and brushed

my hands over my pants to whisk away the flour from the pizza crust I was making, surprised at their trembling. Jace had taken my father to a horse sale in Kolvik and wouldn't be home until suppertime. Neil and Chip were gone—moving James out.

Two days ago, James told my brothers he would be moving back to his old house. Chip and Neil passed this information on to me with a hurt look, like it was all my fault and, maybe, in a way it was. James had kissed me three times now and the last time, he had made it pretty clear how he felt.

I wished I was as clear about what I wanted as I used to be. I didn't think it was fair that as soon as I had made up my mind and figured that the Lord had sent me a clear indication of support by sending Mrs. Woytowich and a job, that I should now renege on my plans.

Because everyone else was gone, the only person who could now be at my door, was the man who had sent my well-ordered plans into a tailspin.

Please, Lord, don't let me make a fool of myself, I prayed as I wiped my hands on a cloth, swallowed down my nervousness and walked to the door.

The man standing on the porch wasn't
James.

It was Les Steglund.

Today he didn't wear a suit. But his
blazer, polo shirt and khaki pants gave him
an air of subdued sophistication that was a
direct contrast to the truck engine sitting on
blocks he stood beside. Chip had put the
engine by the porch and the tires from the
same truck he had leaned up against them.
He and Jace had plans to rebuild it but for
now there was no room in the shop. So, for
some reason that only made sense to my
brothers, it ended up as a lawn ornament
giving the house that whole redneck look
that all the best landscapers were showcas-
ing this year.

"Hello," I said, my voice still breathless
from my previous thoughts. "Would you like
to come in?" I was glad to see him, yet
puzzled. Why had he come all the way out
here. For a date?

Les smiled at me and nodded. "Thank you.
I'd like that."

As I stepped aside, I caught a flash of light.

James stood by his truck, holding a box
with a mirror in it. He stopped, as if he sensed

me watching him. My heart started up again as he stared directly at my house, looking at me, then Les. He nodded slowly, as if to say "Okay then" or something like that, then he chucked his chin at me in a mocking gesture. He shoved the box into the cab of the truck, then got in and slammed the door. As the sound ricocheted across the yard he turned on the truck, and spun it backward in a half circle, then peeled out of the yard, spitting gravel.

"Neighbor," I said succinctly. "He has anger management issues."

"I see." But his puzzled frown told me otherwise.

I opened the door, then kicked aside Neil's cowboy boots so Les wouldn't trip over them. The porch had seemed, to my eyes, passably clean a few moments ago, but when Les entered it with his immaculate clothing and his barbered hair, it suddenly looked messy and dirty.

The kitchen passed muster though, but only because Mrs. Woytowich had spent the morning cleaning it up for me.

"Would you like some coffee?" I asked, banking my burning questions about his presence.

"That would be nice." He settled onto a kitchen chair and glanced around the room. "This is a cozy house."

"Thanks. My dad and brothers built it a number of years ago." I felt a catch in my throat when I thought of my mother's joy in planning the house and how she had only a few months to enjoy it before she died.

"Wow. That's impressive. They did a great job. I like the little breakfast nook."

I glanced over my shoulder at the half-round nook with its low windows overlooking what used to be the garden. There was no table or chair in there and for the first time since the house was built, I wondered why not. It was one of those things that grew on you until you didn't even stop to think that it could be different.

"So you're probably wondering why I'm here," Les said, folding his hands on the table in front of him.

"I'll bite," I said, filling the kettle and putting it on the stove.

"I wanted to tell you in person that you got the job." He waited a beat to let this sink in.

And sink it did. Right to the bottom of my stomach.

It had really happened. I repeated the words to myself to make them real. "Well, that's great," I stammered, trying to absorb this.

"We're really pleased to have you on board. I think you'll be a great asset to our company." He was quiet as I ground the coffee beans, then when I had poured the coffee in the french press and put out some of Mrs. Woytowich's cookies, I was ready to give him some attention.

"I'm curious why you drove out here to tell me," I said, deciding to head directly to "Go."

Les toyed with the napkin I had placed in front of him. "I guess I was wondering why you didn't call me." He looked up at me as he leaned back in his chair, stroking his clean-shaven chin with one hand. "I thought you might. I have to confess I was a bit disappointed."

I frowned, trying to catch his drift. "I haven't been in the city," I said, groping my way around this unusual conversation.

"Did you need an excuse?" His smile deepened his dimples.

"Well, call me old-fashioned, but I always thought it was the man that did the calling and the women who did the washing of hair and filing of nails while waiting for the call," I joked, wishing I could muster up a bit more savoir faire. Which, of course, was a little hard to pull off wearing an apron that hung past my knees and with my hair drifting out of the ponytail I had pulled it into a few moments ago. He'd caught me off guard, not a comfortable position for me.

"I wish I'd known that," Les said, tilting his head to one side, examining me. "I would have."

The timing of this come on really bit. A few months ago I would have been ecstatic to have a good-looking man making hints about dating me. Now, it made me ill at ease.

"About this job," I said, pouring him a cup of coffee. "When did you want me to start?"

"Dan and I were hoping you could begin in a week."

A week? My eyes flew to the calendar. Every day was filled with obligations and appointments. My day timer looked the same.

"That's a bit soon," I stammered, sitting down and pulling my own cup of coffee closer. "I don't know if I can leave my current job that quickly." I had promised Laurel I would go with her to the health nurse, who—according to Laurel—was overbearing and rude. I wanted to see Kent's story get the rare happy ending I saw in this business. I still hadn't found a home-care worker for Stan Bowick and I had a couple of home-studies to finish up.

And James…

"We could give you two weeks," Les continued, as if sensing my hesitation. "Out of courtesy for your current boss."

Could I up and leave in the middle of all my work, knowing that Casey, odious as he might be, would be even more short-handed? Even two weeks wouldn't be enough to wrap up my current case load.

You knew this was coming. There will never be a good time.

I chewed my lip, thinking.

This is what you wanted, isn't it?

Was it my imagination or did my alter ego sound slightly sarcastic?

And why was I not surprised when I heard another knock on the door. I excused myself, got up to answer it. Again my heart started up. Again it wasn't James at the door.

Instead, the person standing on my doorstep was Robin, her mascara running in brown rivulets down her cheek, sobbing her heart out.

Chapter Twelve

"Where's my baby and where's James?" she cried out as soon as I opened the door. She caught me by my shoulder, grabbing onto me, as if afraid I was going to disappear, as well. "The house is empty and that crib…" She sucked in a breath. "The crib is empty, too. Did my brother take off with her? Where did he go?"

"He's moving today." I could see she was terrified and didn't need a lecture on "if you wouldn't have abandoned your baby with your older brother you might have known what was going on in her life." I sensed now was not the time. Such a pro, I am. "He's probably got Sherry with him."

"Where is he moving? Why is he moving?"

He's moving because he doesn't want to see me every day. He's moving because he's angry with me. Which, being the soul of discretion, I kept to myself.

"The place he's moving to isn't far from here. Do you want to come in and wait for him?"

Robin sniffed, sucked in a shaky breath and nodded, palming her mascara off her cheeks. "Yeah. That'd be nice."

I introduced her to Les. He got a trembling smile, but then Robin spied the breakfast nook. "Can I pull a chair into there to watch?"

"Sure. Do you want some coffee or anything?"

"No. I just want to know where my baby is." She grabbed a chair by the back, dragged it to the nook and sat down, twisting her hands around each other. "I'll just sit here, 'kay?"

It wasn't really "'kay," not with Les here, but I nodded. "He'll be back soon. I'm sure of it."

I poured Les a cup of coffee, then he opened his blazer and pulled out a long, white envelope. "I have here the offer of employment and the contract that we like our future employees to sign. I took the liberty of bringing it along for you to see."

I refocused my attention from Robin and her brother, to Les. My hands were shaking as I took the letter. I now held my future in my hands. This had been my focus for the past few months. The vision that had pulled me through my frustrating moments with my brothers and my father and my boss and my work.

It represented a new future—in the city—away from Preston.

But instead of tearing the envelope open, I set it beside my coffee cup. It was good news. It could wait.

"The letter sets out the terms of employment, benefits package, all that," Les said helpfully, glancing from the letter to me. I could see he didn't understand why I wasn't ripping it open, either. "So how soon can you move to the city?" he said, pressing the point.

"I'd need to find an apartment…" I let my voice trail off as I glanced around the kitchen, thought of my cozy bedroom and how excited I had been to have a real bedroom instead of the curtained-off space I'd shared with Chip for the first ten years of my life.

"We could help you with that."

"Why would you want to move to an apartment?" Robin put in from her corner of the kitchen. "They suck. There's never enough space. You've got a great place here, why would you want to move to the city?"

Now I was getting advice from a young woman who thought nothing of leaving her baby daughter with her brother and taking off to who knows where and only phoning once.

I leveled her a blank look. She cut her eyes away from me, as if she understood my unspoken thoughts. "Besides, James wouldn't like it if you moved away."

Her words hung in the air like a faint challenge.

"Is James your brother?" Les asked me, thankfully ignoring Robin's little comment.

"No, James is *my* brother." Robin looked at him, suspicion narrowing her eyes. "He likes Danielle," she said, throwing the words down like a challenge.

I stifled a groan. Why did she think Les Steglund, good-looking man, future coworker, potential date, needed to know that?

And how did she know that?

"James is a good guy." Robin got up from her chair and stood beside me. "I shouldn't have left Sherry with him. I know that."

Robin dropped into a chair and caught my hand, her expression entreating me to understand. "She cries a lot, and I didn't know what to do with her. When I found out I was pregnant, I was going to get rid of her. But James talked me out of it. So when I was having problems I thought it was his idea, he could take care of her. So I left her with James. I had a friend say I could come and stay. But not with Sherry. I couldn't do it—take care of her. You know? I didn't mean to mess up his plans." She squeezed my hand, hard, emphasizing her point. "I miss my baby, so much it hurts and I'm sorry I took off, but I didn't know what to do anymore. I was all alone and I was scared I was going to hurt her. I'm glad James took care of her. He's the best brother in the world, Danielle."

That I could agree with. I couldn't think of too many brothers who would be willing or able to take care of an infant niece. In spite of James's initial anger with his sister, never once did I hear him complain. In fact, if anything, he was almost overprotective. And now I find out that he had convinced her to keep her baby, as well.

A good man.

The words gently sifted through my mind, then settled light as a feather.

A good man. A good guy.

Les cleared his throat, then reached over and took the letter from me. He slit it open with his pinky, pulled out the letter and laid it on the table. "I'm going to need you to sign this for me so that we can start processing your information. For our payroll department."

I bit my lip as I looked down at the letter. Robin clung to my hand. I felt suspended between two places and didn't know which way to go.

I looked at Les, who was watching me now, a puzzled frown creasing his forehead. The letter lay on the table between us. Ominous. Waiting. "How soon do I need to give you my answer?" I asked.

His frown deepened. "I suppose we could wait a few days. Though I was under the impression you hoped to begin as soon as possible."

"I…I have a few cases I'm going to need to clear up that will take a little longer than I had thought."

"Why don't you tell me what you'll need."

I bit my lip. What did I need? How long would it take? I really had no idea. And while I was hesitating, I heard the noise of a truck returning.

Robin saw him the same time I did. "James is back."

I didn't think he would be back this soon, but sure enough, there he was. And he was striding toward the house. Without Sherry.

He knocked on the door, but he didn't wait for me and came right in. He stood in the doorway of the kitchen, his eyes flicking from me to Robin, who had jumped up from the table.

"James, you're here." Robin ran to him, then stopped. "Where's Sherry? Where's my baby? What did you do with her?" Her voice grew more hysterical with each question.

James caught her by the shoulders and gave her a light shake. "Robin, relax. Sherry is sleeping at the other place. Neil is with her now."

Robin gave a shuddering sob. Just like Sherry. "I thought she was gone. I'm sorry I took off and let you take care of her. I'll be a good mother. I will."

James pulled her to him and stroked her

head, and I felt a tug of jealousy. "I know you will, Robin, and I want to help you do it."

She pushed herself away and then looked back at me and Les. James followed the direction of her gaze. "Thanks for letting me stay here, Danielle," she said. "And I hope you like your new job."

James lowered his hands, his eyebrows shooting together. "New job?"

Robin sniffed and nodded. "Yeah. That guy over there—" she chucked her chin in Les's direction "—he's Danielle's new boss."

"Coworker," Les corrected, getting to his feet.

I guess now I had to introduce them. I stood up, as well, gesturing toward Les. "James, this is Les Steglund. Les, this is James Ashby. He's a friend of my brothers."

The contrast between the two men couldn't have been more extreme. Les, all polished and clean, his cheeks still shining from his close shave, his hair neatly clipped and artfully styled. James, dirty and dusty in his frayed jeans with a hole in the knee, his worn jean jacket, his hair that hung past his collar and the stubble that shadowed his cheeks. The man and the guy.

Except the guy had some hidden depths. A diamond in the rough. And the sight of him made my knees wobbly and my breath shaky.

James's gaze ticked from Les to me, a mocking tilt to his smile. "Only a friend of your brothers? Danielle, I'm disappointed."

So much for hidden depths. I knew exactly what he was up to. He was trying to show Les that there was more between us than I was letting on. He was jealous. The thought sent a light shiver trickling down my neck.

"A very good friend," I conceded.

"And this guy…" James chucked his chin in Les's direction. "He's a friend, too?"

"Coworker," Les repeated, annoyance entering his voice.

"At your new job," James said. "Your neat, tidy and boring job."

"Her new position will have multiple challenges," Les protested. "She will be a valuable asset to our organization."

James didn't even glance at Les. "Danielle's more than an asset," he said, his tone taking on an edge I hadn't heard before.

And, from the surprised look on her face, neither had Robin.

"But I won't deny the valuable part," James

continued. "She's valuable to the people of Preston County, as well. The people who don't have someone to speak for them, or stand up for them. People like Kent and Laurel and many others." He held my gaze as if he was trying to say more. "People like me."

My heart fluttered. I couldn't look away from him. And as our eyes held, something indefinable, but tangible, quivered in the air. The moment held, stretched, and Les, Robin and the entire kitchen slipped away from my conscious thought. I was waiting for the flute to come in, all soft and breathy, and for James to come striding toward me à la Richard Gere in *First Knight,* but then Les cleared his throat and Robin said, "Hey, James. What's going on?" and I crashed back to earth.

I'm going to be leaving. I'm going to be quitting my job and going to the city. That's why this Les guy is here….

Man. Les is a man. James is a guy.

But as James slipped his arm tenderly around his sister and escorted her out of my kitchen, and toward the other house, I realized that distinction meant nothing to me anymore.

An awkward silence followed his departure. I fiddled with the strings of my apron, wondering how to proceed, when the sound of a loudly honking horn pushed away my thoughts. What was this? Grand Central Station?

I ran out the door, thinking of my father. Then my poor overworked heart dropped into my stomach.

A rusted, beaten old truck rocked to a halt inches from the back bumper of Les Steglund's BMW. The door opened and Steve Stinson got out. He hitched the belt of his pants, scratched his chest and looked around, taking stock. Then his beady eyes zeroed in on me and he smiled—an oily, greasy, stomach-turning grin. "Well, well, there you are." He hitched his pants again and sauntered over. King of his domain.

I was wondering how long it would be before he came here. He had scattered enough threats around that I was actually surprised it hadn't happened sooner.

"Where's your brother, Chip?" he asked, taking slow deliberate steps up the stairs. He stopped at the top one, rested his hands on his hips and grinned at me.

My stomach flipped but I faced him down. Don't show fear. Don't blink. Be the tough girl your brothers and James seem to think you are.

"What do you want, Steve?" I kept my voice firm, pushing my innate fear of him down.

"Ooh. Aren't we the little banty hen." He laughed shortly and then looked past me. "And here's the rooster, a different one than before. You've been a busy little hen."

"What...do...you...want?" I asked putting hard emphasis on each word.

Steve's grin abruptly shifted to a sneer and he came toe to toe with me. "I...want... to...teach...Chip... a...lesson."

My breath fluttered in my throat. Steve was sober this time and now I was scared stiff.

"Hey, I think you should leave," Les said from behind me.

Steve glanced at him, laughed, then turned back to me. "Pretty boy says I should leave. But I don't want to." He grabbed me by the arm and gave me a shake. "Tell me where Chip is."

I jerked my arm back, but Steve was stronger than I thought. "I'll call the police, Steve."

In the corner of my eye I saw Les move toward him, but one glare from Steve stopped him dead. He turned back to me. "And how are you going to call the cops with me hanging on to you, sugar?"

I gave another ineffectual jerk, wondering

how this stand-off was going to end. Though I had faced down many belligerent parents, uncles, even grandparents, none had ever laid a hand on me. I tried to think, tried to plan, but couldn't. And Les wasn't being much help.

"Let me go, Steve. This is only making things worse." Plus he was cutting off the circulation of my dialing hand.

"Worse for you, hon. So far, I'm doing fine."

"But not for long, Steve."

James's voice was quiet but it resonated.

Relief made my bones weak as James walked up the steps, his booted feet ringing out on the boards. "Let her go, Steve. Now."

Steve glanced from James to me, then back again. "Oh, yeah. I remember you. You're the other guy." Steve looked at Les. "Did you know about this one?" he asked Les, chucking his chin toward James. "Little Miss Danielle here's been seeing him, too. Saw them together by the river, all nice and cozy a while back."

"Thanks for the update, Steve," James said, smiling now. "Now get your hands off Miss Hemstead or I'll have to help you along."

"Like you did then? Lots of guys here. Lots of talk, but no action." Steve gave my arm a shake. I pushed at him and then, before I could even register what had happened, Steve was jerked away from me. James twisted him onto his back on the porch. Steve stared with shock and surprise up at James, who still smiled and now had his booted foot on Steve's chest.

"I think you've stayed long enough, Steve," James said pleasantly.

Steve wasn't smiling. In fact, to my surprise, he looked scared. James waited a beat, to make his point, then took his foot away. Steve scrambled to his feet, sidled past James and scurried back to his truck. Seconds later he was off the yard and gone. Just like that.

I drew in a trembling breath and James turned to me. "You okay?"

I nodded, though my legs shook and wobbled. James glanced at Les. "Get her inside, though I don't think Steve will be back."

And then he was gone again.

I turned down Les's offer of support. I made my own way back into the house, insisting that I was fine, still surprised at how quickly and efficiently James had dealt with Steve.

Les finished his coffee, made small talk

about the job, encouraged me to call him if I needed help finding an apartment and then he scampered off. He was probably wondering what kind of loony person would show up next.

I gathered up the coffee cups, my hands still shaking from my close call with Steve. What would I have done if James wasn't here? I thought again of how James had handled him. Nothing drastic, nothing dramatic, but he got the point across and, better yet, Steve looked spooked.

Thank You, Lord, I prayed, dropping the cups in the sink. *Thank You for James.*

I started washing up, trying to gather my still scattered wits, my mind going backward over the events of the afternoon. In spite of my encounter with Steve, though, other things resonated through my head. James telling Les that I was valuable. To him. Why had he said that?

You know why. He said before that he cares about you. When you and he had your couple's spat.

We weren't a couple. We had kissed a few times. That first time…I let my mind drift back, reliving the touch of his lips on mine, how his eyes glowed, what his hair felt like…no that was the second time…when I brought Sherry to the arena…but he didn't kiss me then…he just…

Ice water running over my hands broke my daydream and with a shake of my head, I switched the water to hot, rinsed off the cups and put them in the dishwasher.

I'd made plans to do some baking, but I was feeling out of sorts from the past hour's events. Steve. Les's coming.

James.

I yanked off my apron, threw it on the kitchen table, retreated to my bedroom, fell backwards on my bed and stared up at the ceiling, wondering why my life was such a frayed and rough business. I had foolishly thought I had solved all my problems, but somehow my life's focus had shifted and my solutions had created more problems.

I liked James.

I more than liked James. I loved how he took care of his sister. I loved how he took care of his niece. I loved how he took his responsibilities seriously. How he'd rescued me just now.

I loved him.

Couldn't. He'd only been a part of my life for a short while.

I loved him.

I thought again of what James had told me about finding contentment in the "now." Was I really living a negative? Was I only thinking about leaving because it was easier than staying and dealing with what I had right now?

Did I really like the challenges my current life gave me? Did I really want to move away from Tracy, from my brothers?

From James?

I love him. The words circled back again and again growing louder each time.

I pushed myself up and, as I often did when struggling with the big or small issues of my life, pulled my Bible off my bedside table. I started randomly flipping it and reading. Grazing. Seeking. My eyes fell on an underlined passage in the Psalms, my preferred destination when I needed comfort or assurance.

Trust in the Lord and do good; dwell in the land and enjoy safe pasture. Delight yourself in the Lord and He will give you the desire of your heart.

The words from Psalm 37 resonated through my tired and confused mind. I closed my eyes and pressed my hand to my face. "Dear Lord, I don't even know what the desire of my heart is anymore," I whispered. "I'm confused and mixed up and I thought I knew what I wanted, but now I don't know."

I waited a moment, waiting for a divine revelation, but all I felt was a sense of coming to the top of a scary roller-coaster ride, waiting for the free fall. Was that fear I was feeling or the exhilaration I felt when I took Spook out? Were the two closely related?

I imagined myself living here, with my brothers and my father, with them clinging to me, I thought of Casey and his endless demands and I panicked, I imagined myself moving to the city, starting over, making new friends. Leaving James. I panicked again. Either scenario was fraught with problems and difficulties.

I didn't know what I wanted.

I wanted to serve the Lord. I wanted to delight in Him. To do good. I wanted to be with James.

"Show me what to do, Lord. Please," I breathed. "I don't know anymore. Help me to seek You first. To serve You first. To let go of all the other stuff and put You first."

* * *

Monday morning at the office. The social workers and caseworkers were all gathered in the meeting room for our weekly meeting and update. We had gone through some of the more difficult cases and tossed some ideas around.

"I don't know what to do with this girl," Henry said in his patent nasally whine. "She won't listen to the foster parents and they don't know how to handle her. I think this case needs further investigation."

Casey nodded, balancing a pencil between his fingers. "Danielle, maybe you could look into that. Before you leave."

I thought of all the things I had to do. Before I left. I thought of the cases that I knew I wasn't going to have time to handle properly. I imagined them going to either Oden, or Henry or Annette, or any of the other workers. I glanced around the room, then at Casey.

"No," I said, my voice crisp and no-nonsense. "I won't do it."

Casey's eyes widened a fraction. "What do you mean?"

"I've got a full caseload. I'm not taking on any more." I held his gaze, remembering a moment when I had gotten my brothers to do the dishes. I wasn't exactly "woman, hear me roar," but professionally I had nothing to lose. I had another job waiting for me. As I held his shocked gaze, I couldn't stop the faint smile teasing my lips. "And while we're at it, I think you need to look at hiring at least two more caseworkers and getting rid of some of the dead wood around here."

A gasp, a stifled cough and Casey's eyes got wider.

"You're out of line, Miss Hemstead."

"Actually, I think I'm right on the line and you've been pushing me over it for the past seven months." I held his gaze. "I was too concerned about doing my best job, about being indispensable and a good worker that I forgot one of the skills of being a good worker is the ability to say no. And for your sake, and mine, I'm saying it now. No. I'm not going to cover for Henry anymore. I'm not going to take the cases that you don't want to give to the other workers because you know I'll say yes. I'm not going to work myself into a nervous breakdown while I keep hoping you'll see what I'm doing and tell me to slow down. Because you're not.

The more I take on, the more you give me and, as I said, that's my own fault. I wanted to be a good social worker, to be needed and while that's a noble cause, I was going about it wrong. James was right. It's up to me and I'm saying *no*."

This little speech would have been a good time to tell my fellow workers about my new job, but I didn't. It had been a week since Les had come to my house with the letter and in that time I still hadn't given Les or Dan a firm decision or turned in my resignation. James had moved off the yard, and I hadn't heard anything from him, either.

I was in limbo. Waiting for something. Maybe to figure out what the desires of my heart were, though I had a clearer idea of what they might be. I knew I couldn't expect some miraculous sign from God, but at the same time a quiet, still voice told me to wait. That hurry and worry are tools of the devil.

And now, facing Casey down, something grew and changed within me. I wasn't waiting for people around me to do what I wanted anymore. I wasn't waiting for them to pick up on clues. I was making myself very, very clear. I was woman, hear me say no.

"I hope you realize the ramifications of what you are doing," Casey said.

"I have no idea what the ramifications are, Casey," I said innocently. "Why don't you tell me?"

His face grew purple and the words A is for Airway, B is for Breathing, C is for Circulation flashed through my head.

But he kept breathing.

Then, to my complete amazement, Casey hunched over the files and glanced at Henry. "You might have to rethink your approach on this one," was all he said.

I allowed myself a tiny smile of victory as I looked down at my case files. And behind that moment of victory slipped the thought, "why hadn't I done this before?"

Because I wasn't ready to let go of control and this desire to be needed. Because I was afraid.

I thought of James then. Thought of how he had pushed me to push my brothers. What he taught me with that. How he had showed me another side of God. Another way of seeing His power and strength.

A nudge of pain followed the memory of James. I hadn't heard from him in a week. In the evenings I joined my brothers and father, watching televised sports, so I could be close to the phone when it rang. But James didn't call and his silence hurt more than any pain I'd experienced before.

I heard the progress of the shop via my brothers. They were getting excited and James was getting some restoration business already. He would do well, they predicted. I heard that Robin had moved in with him and that James was in the process of getting her a job. A good brother, I thought. A good man. A great guy.

My heart stuttered at the memory of him. How easily I could recollect his eyes, how they crinkled at the corners when he smiled, the hint of teasing in every smile, how his eyes got dark before he kissed me.

I missed him. I needed him.

My pen fell out of my hand at that thought and I glanced around to see if anyone else noticed my mind wandering but they were all intently taking notes. I glanced down at mine, and to my dismay noticed that I had scribed out the letter "J" in the margins of my notebook and embellished it. A wishful doodle? Or an internal signal that I would do well to pay attention to.

I struggled through my day, dealing competently with my cases, but I knew my mind wasn't fully engaged. I stayed only fifteen minutes longer, finishing up and when I left, my head aching from the indecision.

But as I put away the papers of my latest case I knew I wasn't going to be leaving. I was going to help Laurel through with her problems, I was going to stay involved with Stan and his family. I wasn't going to be leaving anyone in the lurch.

And I was going to find James and tell him how I felt. What would happen from there? That was up to the Lord.

I felt a clutch of fear and dread and as I walked to the car, I felt the exhilaration of the roller coaster slowly peaking and heading down. Raindrops spittered on my windshield and I had to turn my wipers on, streaking the dust in wide, long smears. I knew I was out of windshield washer fluid and had forgotten to fill it up. On a whim I tried it anyway and, to my surprise, blue liquid streamed out of the wipers, creating a crystal clear arc of clean windshield. One of the boys must have filled it I thought. Guys. I took it as a positive sign and though my stomach was clenched in knots, I felt a lightness in my heart I hadn't felt for months.

Fifteen minutes later I turned down the road where James now lived. As the rain-drops came down, I wondered if they'd gotten the leaky roof fixed.

James's truck wasn't parked in front of the house and my heart thudded with heavy dis-appointment. I didn't know what I was going to say to him, only that I wanted to see him again. To test these awkward feelings.

I was attracted to him. He was appealing on many levels. We had fun together. He made me mad. He hadn't been completely honest with me. We fought.

I missed him. I wanted to see him again. I loved him. There were those words again. And behind them came fear. What if he didn't feel the same? I almost turned the car around. But I had started this wild ride, and I was going to see it through to the end.

Then the front door of the house opened and there he was. My foot came off the ac-celerator and my mouth went dry.

James stood in the lee of his porch, then put his hands on his hips as I pulled into the yard. A classic guy pose that pushed my heart against its rib cage.

I parked the car, turned it off and slowly got out.

He didn't move.

"Hey, there," I said, my voice shaky with nerves, with anticipation, with all the giddy things that girls feel when they see the guy they're thinking about. "Just thought I would stop by. See how Robin is doing."

Now who's being the liar?

"She's not here. She's doing some grocery shopping."

That's why his truck was gone.

"I see." I folded my hands in front of me—a schoolgirl pose—and tapped my thumbs together, stuck for what to say next. I was getting damp but didn't want to get back in the car and didn't feel right in asking to go into James's house.

"When do you leave for your city job?" He took a few steps nearer to my car.

"I'm not going." I gave him a wavery smile and took a step closer myself. Two adults playing "Mother, May I" as rain spittered down. Except without the cumbersome asking.

"I thought you had everything all planned."

"I thought I did, too." I swallowed, took another step closer. I was starting to get wet but couldn't stop this now. "I, well, didn't count on other things happening."

James inclined his head. Took another step. "What things?" One more step.

He was still too far away. I couldn't see his eyes. So I took a few more steps. Close enough to touch. My hand was trembling as I laid it gently on his arm and my heart trembled as I felt the warmth of his skin under his now damp shirt.

"Everything, actually." I could see the gold flecks in his eyes now. Could see faint lines fanning out from his eyes. Could see a slight scar above one eyebrow. I touched it, wondering where it came from, and James caught my hand.

"What are you doing, Danielle?" His voice was gruff but not from anger. I could see he was as moved and as confused as I was. Or used to be.

"I'm trying to make a connection," I said softly. "Trying to tell you what I want."

"So you know now?"

I swallowed as his other hand rested on my waist, pulling me even closer. I nodded.

"I want to stay here. I want to try to take charge of the life I'm living and I want to do it with you."

"But I'm a guy. The enemy."

"You're a guy that I love."

James looked at me a moment, then a smile crawled across his lips. "Are you sure?"

I nodded and then, suddenly, his mouth was on mine, his hands were wrapping themselves around me, holding me hard, tight and close.

I clung to him, holding him, relishing in the strength of his arms. Then, after a long, wonderful moment, he drew back, but he still held me.

"What made you change your mind?" he asked, his rough fingers slipping through my damp hair, brushing it gently back from my face. Just like he had on our "first date." He brushed a few droplets of moisture off my face. We should seek shelter, but I didn't want to break the moment. Thunder rumbled overhead but still we stayed outside.

"Everything," I said. "The other day, when you came to get Robin from the house... when Steve stopped by..."

His hand tightened on my shoulder. "I

wanted nothing more than to plant my fist in his oily face. Just like I wanted to the first time I saw him."

I frowned at him, distracted by his angry words. "First time?"

The anger slipped off his face and he smiled. "Our first date, remember? He came up to you making threats. And I had to be all manly and Schubert-loving, when all I wanted to do was haul back and plow him."

In spite of the emotions that had swirled around us still, I laughed. "That's not very Christian of you, James."

"I know. That's why I only tripped him the other day." His smile faded away and his eyes held mine, serious now. "I was afraid for you. I'm glad I was around."

I thought of Les, standing behind me, being all manly and Schubert-loving. "I'm glad you were, too." I reached up and touched the scar above his eyebrow. "You make me feel safe even though I still think, sometimes, you're a bit dangerous." Thunder crackled above us, as if underlining my comment.

"Not to you."

I shook my head. "Only where my heart is concerned."

"Your heart?" he asked, his voice growing soft and teasing. "How?"

I pulled his head down to mine and kissed him, then pulled back. "Like that." I smiled at him, letting my feelings for him flower, grow, come to fruition. Whatever it was that deep feelings do when they're acknowledged.

And as James gave me another kiss, the skies opened in earnest now and the rain came sheeting down.

His lips felt warm against my cold skin, then slowly he pulled away. He smiled down at me, water running down his face. "I love you, Danielle Hemstead. I want to spend the rest of my life trying to figure you out."

His words sang through me like, well, like a Schubert composition. What had James said? Long melodies, both brusque and leisurely. Come to think of it, that described James to a T.

"I love you, James." I had to raise my voice so that it could be heard over the sound of the rain clattering on the roof and puddling on the ground. "More than I thought I could ever love anyone." I pulled his head down and in spite of the fact that we were both getting soaked to the skin, gave him a long, leisurely kiss.

James pulled back, stroked my streaming hair from my face. "Come inside," he urged. "We need to get out of the rain."

I shivered then, as the cold finally seeped through my wet clothes.

We ran up the path to the house. Inside he directed me to the bathroom and handed me some of Robin's clothes. I dried myself off as best as I could, cleaned my running mascara and brushed my hair. The drowned rat look, I thought. Then I laughed. I somehow don't think James cared.

When I came out of the bathroom, he had changed, as well. Blue jeans. Corduroy shirt. Looking good.

"Do you want some coffee or tea?" he asked.

I shook my head and, with the confidence of a woman who knew her man, I walked toward him and slipped my arms around him. Just because I could and because I wanted to. I looked around the house. It was even cozier than the one on the farm. He had a knack, that was for sure. Then something occurred to me and I pulled away from his warm embrace.

"Did you get the roof fixed?" I asked.

He frowned. "Roof?"

"Yeah. You moved to the house on the farm because it was leaking." I looked around the room. No pails out. Up at the ceiling. No water spots. "You must have gotten it fixed otherwise you wouldn't have moved Sherry and Robin in here." I narrowed my eyes at his puzzled expression and things became clear. "Don't tell me. The roof doesn't leak."

James pulled me close and gave me another kiss, but I wasn't going to be that easily distracted.

"If this was another one of my brothers' schemes…" I warned.

James's kiss stopped me. "Actually," he admitted in a sheepish voice, "this one was all mine. After that first date, I wanted to see you again and when you came to the riding arena you were so ticked off, I knew the only way that was going to happen was if I moved closer. So I exaggerated the leaking roof story. It leaks all right. Just not that much."

"But there was no bet."

He brushed another kiss over my lips. "There was no bet. That's the truth. Meeting you in the restaurant happened exactly like I told you. Me moving to your old house…

well, that was my idea. And you have to admit, it was a good one."

I held up my hand. "Please, please don't tell me that Robin and Sherry were part of this, as well."

"No. No, and definitely no." He sighed and shook his head. "That was completely unrehearsed, unplanned and unwelcome."

"I don't know. I kind of liked taking care of Sherry," I said.

"Well, if Robin sticks around, you might be able to more than you want. I'm still working on the whole responsibility thing."

I smiled up at him, gave his arm a squeeze. "You're a wonderful brother. My own could take a few lessons from you."

"Your brothers have their own strengths. They just need a little guidance."

"Just like Robin."

James pulled me into his arms again. I was liking this whole getting to know each other thing. "So we can help each other, then."

"Yeah. We can." I pulled his head down and gave him a long, slow kiss. And afterward, as we sat together on the couch, making plans for our future, I let a prayer of thankfulness drift up. Thankfulness for James.

Gentle yet firm. Safe yet dangerous.
A man in the best sense of the word.
My man.

* * * * *

Next month brings another special
Steeple Hill Café novel in Love Inspired!
Watch for MY SO-CALLED LOVE LIFE
by Allie Pleiter
On sale August 2006.

Dear Reader,

My husband is a guy. I've come to accept this over time, but even more importantly, come to appreciate the very guyness of him. I have learned that though he doesn't buy me flowers regularly or jewelry or tell me he's thinking of me or cook dinner regularly, he does tell me he loves me, gives me a hug when he comes home from work smelling like diesel and sawdust, reads his Bible with conviction, telephones our children and his mother every Sunday and is available when bats need to be chased out of the house and mousetraps need to be emptied. He loves our children, loves the Lord and lives his life in his own plain, simple way. With this book, I wanted to show that sometimes we women have romantic ideals that very few mortal men can live up to, but if we take the time, we can learn to see the good things the guys in our lives can give us. I know Richard has taught me generosity, appreciation of nature and, at times, has pushed me out of my comfort zone and challenged me to get that horse down that rocky slope, chase that cow that won't pay attention, or drive that loud, noisy machine that gives me the heebie-jeebies. At the same time, I know he's learned from me. God has blessed us in our marriage, and I'm thankful for how we've grown together in our faith and in our love. I hope that those of you who are married can appreciate the good things about your husband, and those of you who aren't, can learn to see past some of the *guy* behaviors that can sometimes mask a tender heart.

Carolyne Aarsen

P.S.: I love to hear from my readers. You can contact me at caarsen@telusplanet.net, or visit my Web site at www.carolyneaarsen.com.

QUESTIONS FOR DISCUSSION

1. Danielle has a preconceived notion about guys versus men. What is your take on that notion?

2. How would you describe the perfect man? What would he look/act like to you?

3. James makes the statement that most guys don't know what women want. Do you think that's true? Why or why not? Are we women so hard to understand?

4. What *do* we want? Is it attainable?

5. John Eldredge's book *Wild at Heart* has struck a chord in many men and seems to have spawned a new movement. He makes the statement that church has served to make men more like women and not allowed some of their innate wildness to come to the fore. Do you think that's true? Why or why not?

6. In what ways have you been guilty of judging a person based on a first impression? How long does that impression linger?

7. Sometimes we want the men in our lives to anticipate our wants, and then get upset because they don't. Is this wrong? What are some of the unrealistic expectations people can have about the men in their lives?

8. God has created a variety of men and women. How can we learn to set aside our own notions of how Christians should behave and learn to see Christ in others?